Chloe King has

~~9 Lives~~

8

7

6

5

4

3

2

1

the nine lives of chloe king

The Fallen

The Stolen

The Chosen
(coming soon)

the nine lives of chloe king

VOLUME TWO

The Stolen

by
CELIA THOMSON

SIMON PULSE
New York   London   Toronto   Sydney

First Simon Pulse edition September 2004

Copyright © 2004 by 17th Street Productions, an Alloy company

SIMON PULSE
An imprint of Simon & Schuster Children's Publishing Division
1230 Avenue of the Americas, New York, NY 10020

 Produced by 17th Street Productions,
an Alloy company
151 West 26th Street
New York, NY 10001

Manufactured in the United States of America
10 9 8 7 6 5 4 3 2

Library of Congress Control Number 2004103118

ISBN 978-0-689-86659-3

8/11

Mom,

Keira's grandma just died—I know I've trashed her in the past, but she's really broken up over this. A bunch of us are spending the night at her place; she's there alone while her parents deal with the funeral stuff and the rest of the family. I'll call you tonight.

Love,
Chloe

Prologue

She was back at the Golden Gate Bridge.

Paul and Amy were already gone. The highway spanning the bridge was empty of cars. The water below had stopped. Everything was silent, waiting.

Chloe wasn't surprised when Alexander Smith—the Rogue who'd tried to kill her before—seemed to drop out of the sky, a dagger in each hand. He was saying something but making no sound. She could tell he was going to attack and ducked, but her movements were so very, very slow. . . .

There was a scream as one of his daggers grazed her head. *But that didn't really happen,* she realized, confused. *That's not what happened last time. I was supposed to leap at him.* . . . He was coming at her, two more daggers in his hands, murder in his eyes.

Chloe couldn't make herself move.

But I won this fight, she told herself, panicking. *I've already been through all this and I won—*

The Rogue's arm shot out, dragging a blade across her face. Chloe leapt back just in time. *Did he scratch me? Am I bleeding?*

"Brian!" she called out, knowing her friend was supposed to appear. But wait, wasn't there some confusion? Had he been helping her or the Rogue?

Brian appeared, standing at an impossible angle on the rail. He looked serious and his arms were crossed. "Who is it?" he asked gravely. "Me or Alyec?"

"Help me!" Chloe screamed, trying to run away from the Rogue.

"You cause a lot of trouble," the Rogue said with a faint smile.

Then he drove a blade deep into her belly.

As she fell, she saw Alyec run and leap at Brian.

"No!" she screamed as the two boys went tumbling off the bridge.

The Rogue smiled, his face so close that his sour breath enveloped her. He raised the blade again, this time aiming for her neck.

One

"No!"

Chloe woke up covered in sweat and trembling.

"It was a dream," she said, letting her tense muscles sink back into the bed. She had fought the Rogue a day ago—and she had won, if you could call it that. He had fallen off the bridge when Chloe failed to grab his arm, and now he was the one who was dead. Chloe was okay. Alyec and Brian were both alive. Everything else was just a nightmare.

The room was bathed in a soothing half-light that could have been dawn but somehow *felt* like dusk. She wasn't home; the crisp richness of the bedding and the velvet fringe of the throw someone had tucked around her were definitely alien to the King household. Where *was* she? Slowly it came back to her.

Alyec had taken her to this place after the fight. His leg was injured by one of Brian's throwing stars. Brian had claimed that he was trying to stop them from running deeper into Tenth Blade territory, but Chloe still wasn't sure if that was true. . . . They had taken a taxi; she remembered looking out the window and seeing that they were on the bridge, the beautiful lights of San Francisco receding behind them. When they finally stopped, she was led through pitch darkness up to a house, where a short blond woman greeted and welcomed them, even though it was the middle of the night. She led them through narrow halls and—

Chloe sat up, remembering more from last night.

Something had passed them in one of the halls that still scared Chloe, even now that she was safely tucked in a luxurious bed.

The hall was dark and empty, and then, seemingly out of nowhere, a girl her own age drifted past them, silent as a black ghost. Her eyes gleamed in the low light, green and slit like a cat's. From underneath her straight black hair poked two giant ear tips, pointed, black, and covered with fur. She was gone as quickly and silently as she came.

Chloe had gasped and pointed and Alyec rolled his eyes and explained that the cat girl was just Kim. The other woman nodded nonchalantly. But even that simple explanation didn't make Chloe feel any better. She had no idea where she was or who these people were that Alyec had taken her to.

"I'll come by soon," he had promised after they stopped at a door.

"Go *away*, Alyec," the woman said sweetly, pushing

Chloe into the room. For some reason it was that maternal tone, the nice-but-ordering voice, that had set Chloe at ease again. Wherever they were, there were normal rules and people.

She couldn't see much in the tiny space except for a bed with about a thousand down pillows. She collapsed on it without asking.

"You have a nice little nap," the woman had said, clucking her tongue and pulling a velvet chenille throw up over Chloe's shoulders.

As exhausted as she was, Chloe hadn't been able to fall asleep instantly, and when she had, her dreams had all been nightmares: she was back on the Golden Gate Bridge, fighting for her life against the Rogue, the Order of the Tenth Blade's most lethal—and psycho—assassin. Sometimes in her half dreams Alyec was there, sitting on the side and watching like he had or fighting beside her. Sometimes Brian was there, helping her like *he* had—or chasing her the way she thought he had. Even though it had all really happened, it *still* didn't feel real. But it was.

Now that she was awake, Chloe was *still* tired and without answers to the questions that had been plaguing her nightmares: *Why me? What did I ever do to anyone?*

Chloe noticed a little side table that had been set up next to her while she slept. It was covered with a large doily and on it was a plate with various cold cuts and cheeses, slices of bread, and little cups of mustard and other condiments. A glass—*crystal?*—of water was placed next to a can of Diet Coke.

Chloe made herself the largest sandwich she could manage between two slices of thick brown pumpernickel, slathering it with mustard. It took only about a minute for her to gobble it down, maybe another to toss back the water and the Diet Coke. She let out a mighty burp (then looked around nervously, but no one was there). Somehow she wasn't as frightened as she should have been. Her belly was full, she was in a beautiful room, and she was safe. Strangely, she sort of felt happy.

Chloe looked around: the beams and floor planks were ancient wood, dark and polished just enough to keep the dust away, not so much as to be shiny. The room itself was small but cozy: there was an intricate Oriental rug in dark colors in one corner, on top of which sat a lightly worn velvet armchair. Over its back was another chenille throw. An old-fashioned floor lamp with a slightly cracked marble base and brass upright lit the room with a soft orange glow from three fake candle lightbulbs. If Chloe had the money—and the right house—this was exactly how she would decorate it.

She rose and stretched, feeling her joints and muscles snap into place. *Back to my old self, finally.* She pulled her cell phone out of her back pocket and turned it on. Three-quarters battery left. No one had left her a voice mail, not even her mom. *She must have bought that whole "I'm going over to Keira's" thing,* thought Chloe.

She called Amy and was a little surprised when she didn't pick up—both Amy and Paul had seen the whole Rogue-Alyec-Brian-Chloe mess last night—shouldn't they be worried?

Amy's voice mail beeped.

"Hey, it's Chloe. I'm fine. I'm staying with some . . ." She paused for a moment, trying to think of the right word. "Uh, distant cousins and friends. Don't call—I'm going to keep my phone off for a while. Save the battery. I'm safe, and I'll call you later."

Chloe then left a message for her mom, who wasn't home. "Hey, I'm going to be with Keira for a little longer. . . ."

She heard the sound of old-fashioned high heels clicking down the hallway outside her room, growing louder as they came closer.

"Um, love you. And, uh, I'll call you later—I'm turning off my phone. Okay, bye."

Chloe quickly shut off her phone and put it away. Soon a woman appeared at her door, finishing up a conversation half in Russian and half in English on a tiny cell phone dangling with charms. It took Chloe a second to realize that she was the same woman from the night before who had taken her to this room, just in more professional clothes.

"Yes," she said. "Two dozen. And tell Ernest thanks for the purple pens. The kids love them. Spaceba." She hung up and gave Chloe a weary smile. "Sometimes I feel more like an office manager than president of this little place. How are you feeling?"

"Uh, fine, thank you . . ."

It was hard to tell how old the other woman was; her body was Tinkerbell perfect, small and curvy with a tiny waist and amazing calves that were highlighted by what looked like six-inch stiletto heels. She had short, elfin blond hair and black eyes. The skirt and jacket suit she wore were a little flashy for Chloe's taste but obviously expensive. There was something more about her, though . . . the way she held her head, the way she stared without blinking, a certain smell that Chloe couldn't put her finger on.

Chloe knew this woman was just like her. A cat person.

"I'm Olga Chetobar," she said, extending a hand with long, perfect nails. One of them had a little golden charm dangling from the end. "I'm president of Firebird's, well, we call it 'human resources' department. We find and rescue, shall we say, *strays* and bring them home."

"Home?"

"Sergei will explain—he's very anxious to meet you." Olga checked something on her phone again.

"Thanks for the—uh, lunch," Chloe said, wondering if it would be rude to ask about a shower, new clothes, or getting in contact with her mom.

"Don't get used to it," the older woman said with a warm smile. "We all pitch in together around here. You will soon, too."

"I don't mean to be rude—it's great here—but when

will I get to go home? I think my mom is going to start to worry."

Olga held up her hand. "Sergei takes care of this. Your mother will be informed that you were witness to a potentially lethal crime—which you *were*—and are in police custody. Or federal witness protection. Or something. Maybe he already told her? I don't know the details—his people always do a good job, though. Come with me now." She looked at her watch, something expensive with gold and diamonds. "He is expecting you."

Chloe pulled on her Sauconys as fast as she could without tying them and followed Olga out of the room. They walked down a dimly lit narrow hallway, possibly the one from the night before. In the daylight she saw that the walls were decorated with reproduction vintage paper with little roses and stripes and things, and the floor was made up of little tiny planks of different-colored wood.

"Sorry we practically put you in the attic," Olga said over her shoulder as her tiny feet rapidly tapped their way toward a narrow stair. "We were a little unprepared and figured you shouldn't be disturbed for a while. This place can get busy and loud during the workweek."

Chloe had to double-time it to catch up, practically tripping down and around two flights of narrow stairs tightly clustered around a center well.

"What *is* this place?"

"Firebird Properties, LLC," Olga said crisply, proudly,

looking at her watch again. "A real estate and marketing company. Mainly we deal with investment and commercial properties, not so much with housing." Olga flowed off the stairs and was halfway down a new hall as she spoke; Chloe had to run to keep up. It was a much more modern area, with gray wall-to-wall carpeting and art prints framed on painted walls.

"Housing? Market? What . . . ?" Suddenly Chloe ground to a halt as she passed a big picture window on her left. She stared out.

They were one floor above ground; the first thing that was obvious was a huge lawn sweeping down, spreading out to the road. When she pressed her face up to the glass and looked directly down, she could see a fountain in the middle of a circular gravel driveway that led gently along one side of the lawn and downhill to the road. There was, as Chloe had guessed there might be, a gate at the end of it.

"This is that house," she said slowly.

"What house?" Olga asked, coming back to look.

"The one that Alyec showed me. When I was depressed. He drove me out somewhere near Sausalito and showed me this incredible house. . . ." It had been a wild day. The fight with Amy, the car that Alyec stole from the senior running back, the way Alyec liked catching air on the San Francisco hills, the escape from the city to see this huge old mansion. From the outside it was all stone and marble and as impressive as a museum.

And now she was inside.

"Alyec took you here?" Olga asked, faintly amused.

"I thought this was someone's house." *Like somebody really rich,* thought Chloe, though she didn't add that part.

"It is. A few of us live here full time besides Sergei. Me, Kim, and Ivan and Simone. But it is also the headquarters for Firebird and for our people. . . . Sometimes it is important to stay out of everyone's way, and this is certainly as nice a place as any. Nicer, even," the older woman reflected without a smile on her mouth, but her eyes danced. Chloe couldn't tell if the lack-of-facial-expressions thing was Russian or a cat-person attribute.

"You mean this is a place where—?"

"*Sergei* will explain," Olga said, shaking her finger. Then she spun and tapped away again. "Come!" she ordered.

Chloe followed.

There were offices in this part of the building, and actual people. It kind of reminded Chloe of her mom's accountant or their dentist, both of whom worked out of retrofitted nineteenth-century Italianate houses. When she was little, Chloe thought they were mansions—they were bigger than her, Amy's, and Paul's houses combined—and mentioned that freely, embarrassing the hell out of her mother.

"Who was that?" Chloe asked after she stepped aside for another person. He was a young, serious-looking man with brown eyes, who gave her a cursory smile as he made his way past her.

"That's Igor, director of sales."

Olga walked Chloe through a lobby with fresh, expensive flower arrangements and real paintings. She spoke rapid-fire Russian with a girl in a gaudy T-shirt with rhinestones and then brought Chloe up to a half-closed mahogany door. It bore a neat brass plaque with the name *Sergei* inscribed on it. It sort of reminded Chloe of a coffin.

Olga knocked at the door and then went in, beckoning Chloe to follow.

Inside was a large, beautifully appointed office whose main feature was a *huge* dark desk in front of bay windows hung with dark green velvet curtains. Behind the desk was a man who at first glance appeared to be far larger than he actually was. His body was extremely square, wide, and short, and so was his head. There were a few lines under his eyes, not quite bags, but he seemed like the sort of man who had gotten handsomer as he got older. His light blue eyes were overshadowed by huge orange-and-silver caterpillar brows.

He looked up from a stack of papers.

"*You* must be *Chloe!*" he boomed happily, throwing the papers down and leaping up. He came around to the other side of the desk in short but powerful strides, approaching her like a steam engine, his arms outstretched.

As ungainly as his build was, the suit he wore fit him

perfectly, immaculately, and, like everything else here, expensively.

"Welcome *home*, kitten!" he cried, giving Chloe a big hug. "Another one home! Another little bird back to the nest!" He kissed her on both cheeks and then held her out at arm's length. His strength was so great and his presence so powerful, Chloe found herself just sort of being manhandled, too stunned to resist.

"Let me see you!"

He looked deep into her eyes and face, examining her. After a moment he looked a little disappointed but tried to cover it with a smile.

"Well, you don't look like anyone I know—but that's even better. A new face is a good thing around here." He flicked her hair back in a paternal fashion. "And so pretty, too!" He chuckled. "We certainly are lucky to have you. I am Sergei Shaddar, leader of the Pride. And pleased as anything you have joined us."

Leader of the Pride? Sergei Shaddar? Suddenly it all clicked: *Sergei*, Alyec's distant relative, who hadn't helped his family emigrate. Owner of the mansion Alyec had brought her to. This mansion. It was all coming together.

"I have sent her records on to the department," Olga said softly.

"Blood work?"

The woman shook her head. "There is no need unless we find some sort of likely jumping-off point."

"A shame. I like the scientific stuff," he confided to Chloe with a grin. "It is so modern. A drop of blood and we know who your parents are! If we knew who your parents were, that is," he added. "So many orphans," he said sadly. "So few whole families left."

"I'm sorry?" Chloe said, trying to understand what exactly he was talking about.

"I'll go," Olga said, nodding—almost deferentially—to Sergei and backing out so that she faced him the entire time. She closed the door behind her.

"Chloe." Sergei put a meaty hand on her own. His short fingers suddenly developed claws, much thicker and shorter than hers. He pressed them against the back of her hand, indenting the skin but not breaking it, and looked at her seriously. "You are a daughter of the Kings of the Hunt. Goddesses were your ancestors. You are Mai. That is what we are called."

"Mai?" Chloe couldn't tear her eyes from his claws and touched them, picking up his hand and turning it over, staring at it in wonder. Sergei let her without questioning.

"People of the Lions. The Desert Hunters. Children of Bastet and Sekhmet."

Chloe vaguely recognized the last two names or at least Bastet—that was the cat pendant Amy always wore. "We're . . . Egyptian? I thought everyone here was from, like, Eastern Europe or something."

"No, originally we're from Egypt and other parts of

Africa. But then again, isn't everyone?" He chuckled. "Our race is thousands of years old, Chloe. We are gifted and different—and there are very few of us left."

"How did you find me?" Chloe felt a little embarrassed asking; he was giving her the lowdown on their history and she was all like, *Okay, but back to me.*

"There was no way of knowing for certain you were one of us." Sergei shrugged. He pulled his hands from her and waved them around as he spoke; the claws made little whistling noises in the air. They slowly retracted back into his fingers. "Usually we . . . show our true nature at adolescence, fourteen or fifteen or so. Alyec mentioned that you seemed . . . *different*, and when we looked up your records, we found out that you were adopted from the Soviet Union—Abkhazia, to be exact. Then we watched you to make sure. Alyec was told to intervene and instruct you in secrecy when things started getting complicated with the Rogue and the Tenth Blade."

A thousand questions were whirling in Chloe's mind.

"Why didn't Alyec just *ask* or something?" she demanded.

Sergei gave her a patient, pitying look. "Chloe King, if you were already upset by things that were going on with you and someone just said, 'Hey, you're secretly a lion woman, there's a whole bunch of us here in San Francisco, join us,' what would you have done?"

Freaked out. She nodded slowly.

17

"We would have speeded up things a lot more if we had known that Alexander Smith was after you and that you were *dating* a member of the Tenth Blade."

"We weren't dating," Chloe mumbled without thinking.

"What?"

"We weren't really dating," Chloe said more loudly. "He wouldn't even kiss me."

"Of course not." Sergei nodded as if this were the most obvious thing in the world. Chloe raised her eyebrow.

"Humans and the Mai can't—ah, how shall I say this. Uh, *mate*," the older man said, coughing in embarrassment. "It kills them. Like we are toxic."

Xavier! The guy she'd picked up at that club the night before her sixteenth birthday. They had made out in the parking lot, and when Chloe felt herself almost overcome with desire, she had left and gone home. Days later she went back to his apartment to see him: he was almost dead, covered in sores where her fingers had raked down his back. Chloe had even called an ambulance for him anonymously.

"Oh my God—" Chloe covered her mouth with her hand. "I made out with a guy at a club, and he totally had to go to the hospital. . . ."

Sergei raised his eyebrows.

"Is he going to die?" she whispered.

"Probably not, if you just kissed him," he said slowly. "But keep this in mind for the future."

Thank God I didn't kiss Brian, Chloe thought, and

then quickly remembered that she had no intention of kissing Brian ever again. *Or seeing him. Or thinking about him,* she thought. It had been a great relationship until the whole revealing-he-was-a-member-of-the-Tenth-Blade-thing. Chloe went over the facts in her head again; she couldn't help it. He'd claimed he was trying to save her from the Rogue at the fight on the bridge—but some of his shuriken had come perilously close to her own head. And then there was the one that he'd neatly buried in Alyec's leg when they were running away. . . . He'd said he was trying to stop them. To protect them from Tenth Bladers hidden in the Marin Headlands. But he never had liked Alyec. . . .

And now Chloe began to understand why.

"Anyway, think of it, Chloe! You have a real family now—people who are related to you by blood and who share your heritage! And you know what?" He pounded his fist on the palm of his other hand, causing Chloe to jump back. "*I'll* sponsor you. You can't live *here* all the time—"

"What about my mother? When can I go back?" Chloe didn't want to offend Sergei, but all of this family talk did bring Chloe's mind back to her mom.

Sergei sighed and shook his head. "Not anytime soon, I'm afraid. The Tenth Blade is trying to track you down. They believe you killed Alexander Smith; the streets are crawling with their agents. If you leave, you will be dead before you get halfway across town."

"Can I call her at least?" Chloe thought it might be best to ask this before admitting that she already had. . . .

"I'm sorry, Chloe, but no. Even if the Tenth Blade hasn't tapped her lines, they are almost certainly monitoring her every move. And if your mom called the police, then her line is *definitely* tapped."

"But . . . won't she be suspicious? Where does she think I am? Oh my God—what are my *teachers* going to think when I don't show up on Monday?"

Sergei ticked off his fingers. "Your mother is being informed that you are part of a federal witness protection program and that she will be allowed to speak with you as soon as it's safe. Your school has been informed that you have come down with mono and will be out for a while." Sergei smiled. "We have even given them an address to send your homework," he added, satisfied with himself.

Chloe flinched. *Did it have to be mono? The kissing disease? Couldn't it have been Ebola or mad cow or something you don't get from sucking face?*

Sergei fixed her with unamused eyes, noticing her reaction. "It is the most logical debilitating sickness for a teenager to come down with."

"It's just that everyone's going to think, well, whatever . . ." Chloe said, resigned.

Everything sucked. She couldn't talk to her mom; she couldn't even tell her mom the truth; the whole school would be laughing at her; and she was stuck here for a while. It wasn't that she wanted to *leave*, precisely, but she wanted the option. And then there was the idea of an entire city blanketed with men who wanted to kill her. Whose purpose was to kill her. Her, Chloe King. Sixteen and harmless.

"I didn't kill him!" she said, the anger in her voice surprising even her. "When he slipped, I tried to *help him back up!*"

"Why would you do that?" Sergei asked, genuinely surprised.

"I don't know, I just . . . I don't know. It seemed like the right thing to do." Chloe shrugged helplessly; she couldn't explain it. *It's just what you do.* "Who are these people anyway?"

"The Tenth Blade exists solely to wipe us out," Sergei said, putting his hands back on her shoulders, a black and serious look in his eyes. "They believe the Mai are evil, sent by the devil or some such nonsense. They only tolerate us here because it is harder to kill people out of hand in America than elsewhere. . . ." His eyes glazed as he thought about another time and place. Then he refocused. "And as long as we don't draw too much attention to ourselves, we are more or less safe." He spat viciously. "We have to hide like *rats* here." He waved his hand around the room, a room that Chloe personally didn't think would be out of place in the White House, much less a place for rats. "They fear our power. We are stronger, faster, and quieter than they—we should be revered, not annihilated."

He was silent for a moment, seething.

"Well, I'm sure Olga is having someone make up a real room for you," Sergei said, lighthearted again in a flash. "I have to go to a meeting now, but you should go to the library and learn the history of our people. Simone and Ivan will be notified about our newest resident. You have complete run of the place. Goodbye, Chloe, and welcome!" He gave her one last bear hug and then ushered her out, pushing her lightly on the back.

"Wait! One more question!" Chloe begged.

"Yes?" He paused just as she was over the threshold.

"Why are so many people here on a *Saturday*?"

"This is *real estate!*" he said as he began shutting the door behind her. "We never really close!"

She just stood there, dazed for a moment, thinking about everything Sergei had said. *Blood tests? Goddesses? Thousands of years old?* A fax beeped somewhere, breaking her reverie. This was a strange place for ancient hunters to gather.

The girl in the ugly, sparkly T-shirt told Chloe how to get to the library and then ignored her.

Chloe wandered off. She felt disoriented and ghostly in this half-modern, half-old place; not properly belonging but somehow connected with it. There was no one around she knew, nothing familiar, yet she was probably safer than she had been anywhere for the past month. A refugee in the home of the people who really were her family. *Her . . . pride . . .* It was all too much, yet so far they all seemed painfully normal. Olga with her cell phone and Sergei with his businessman's attitude. Chloe realized she was expecting them to act secretive and weird, like vampires.

And to *not* be involved with stuff like real estate.

The library, like everything in the mansion, was spectacular and perfect and right out of an English costume drama: built-in wall-to-wall bookshelves, infinitely high windows between parenthetical pairs of infinitely long velvet drapes that were just a touch faded. She walked along one immaculate bookcase, looking at the titles. Most of them were classics or encyclopedias though there was a case devoted to modern books like *Bridget Jones's Diary*. One shelf had a pair of bookends in the form of Egyptian cats—Bastet, Chloe realized, and it *was* the same one on Amy's necklace, a house cat with a slight smile and an earring. The other was a lion with her teeth bared. In between the two were books with titles like *The History of the Mai, Essays on Mai Origins, Res Anthro-Felinis*. Chloe picked one up and flipped through the pages, already bored and intimidated by the old-fashioned font and paragraph-long sentences.

She sighed and threw herself into a chair.

Two

"What do we do *now?*"

Behind them another helicopter was circling the bridge. They had been hovering like pissed-off dragonflies off and on since Friday night. Paul and Amy hoped that the National Guard had caught up to Chloe and whoever was attacking her and split them up—but almost a day had passed, and it didn't look like there had been any resolution.

Paul thought he'd seen a body fall from the bridge, but he didn't say anything about it to Amy.

"Well?" his girlfriend demanded again.

Paul sighed.

"I don't know—what do *you* think we should do?"

"Call her mom . . . ?" But even as she suggested it, Amy trailed off, knowing that it probably wasn't the right thing to do—or, more importantly, that it wasn't what Chloe would want. She ran her hands through her chestnut hair in exasperation, pulling on the roots. It was a leftover habit from when she was younger and tried to flatten her big, often frizzy hair every chance she got. "What do you think it was all about—*really?*"

They'd had this conversation several times in the last twenty-four hours, but somehow Amy was never satisfied with Paul's answers.

"I don't know. Drugs? Gangs? Some weird psycho game of tag?"

"Maybe it's got to do with her real parents or something. Maybe she's actually some sort of Russian Mafia princess."

Paul gave her a lopsided smile. Silently they started to walk home, not holding hands or anything. Like they had in the old days, when the three of them were just good friends. Before Chloe almost died from falling off Coit Tower. Before she and Amy got into that weird little snit they were in for days—and had just patched up. Before Chloe started seeing Alyec and Brian . . .

"You know," Paul said slowly, "a *lot* of weird shit has happened with Chloe in the last couple of months, don't you think?"

Amy shrugged. "Seems to me she got her period and turned into a total bitch. For a while, at least," she added hastily. Chloe might have been a bitch, but she was still Amy's best friend, and she was still missing.

"No, it's more than that." Paul frowned, crinkling his long white forehead. "I mean like her fall and the bruises on her face and her random absences from school—not to mention being totally incommunicado about general Chloe life issues."

"She was going to tell us everything," Amy remembered. "On the bridge . . . She was just about to explain *something*. . . ."

". . .when that freak with knives showed up." They looked at each other for a long moment.

"We were talking about her crush on *Alyec* when she jumped off Coit Tower," Amy suddenly pointed out.

"She didn't jump, she fell," Paul said, surprised at the way Amy said that. She was the only person on the planet who probably knew Chloe better than he did, and it was a really weird thing to say about their friend. At no point in her life, even at her gothiest moments, had Chloe *ever* seemed the suicidal sort. *A jackass, sometimes, but never suicidal.* Jumping up onto the ledge to get more attention had been a *little* rash, but they had been drinking, and it wasn't completely out of the range of typical Chloe behavior.

"Whatever," Amy said quickly, dismissing it. "Her life started going crazy after that. I'll bet it has something to do with him."

"That's insane. How could *thinking* about him have anything to do with getting mugged or whatever?" Paul asked. He tried not to laugh or smile but couldn't stop his dark eyes from twinkling. Fortunately Amy wasn't looking directly at him.

"No! Think about it." She began counting off facts on the tips of her black glitter fingernails. "She was mugged right after we all split up at The Raven, then became a total hag when she started actually dating Alyec—and he's Russian, just like her. Maybe he's got her into something *bad.*"

"What about *Brian*, then?" Paul demanded. "As long as we're accusing random people of having somehow screwed up Chloe's life and sent assassins after her. Brian, the mysterious sort-of boyfriend who never kissed her, who isn't in school, and, most importantly— *who we've never seen?*"

Amy stared at him with blank blue eyes, at a loss for an answer. He was about to add a few more salient facts that proved she was a complete wacko with insubstantial—*crazy*—arguments, but then he noticed Amy's lips trembling and tears forming on her lower lids.

"She'll be okay. The National Guard is out there. We can call the police if you want or her mom later—let's say if we haven't heard from her in a few hours. Okay?"

Amy nodded miserably, and they continued walking home.

Three

Amy looked into the bottom of her locker hopefully. Nope, nothing. She was always making cute little notes for Paul and slipping them into *his* locker. Sometimes they were quick scrawls—*See you in English!*—and sometimes they were really intricate things she made the night before with cloth and her glue gun and stuff.

Not. Once. Had he ever done the same for her. She didn't want to outright *ask*—but how strongly did a girl have to hint? Now that she was finally dating a nice, nonpsycho boy, she figured she should cash in on some of the perks that were supposed to go along with it. She was being stupid, she knew, and selfish: Paul did all other kinds of nice boyfriendy things, like buying tickets ahead of time for movies they wanted to see and getting her a coffee at the café if she asked. And he would talk to her for *hours* on the phone about all sorts of things. . . .

But once, just once, Amy wished someone would treat her exactly the way she wanted them to. All that stuff about the Golden Rule and karma and stuff—her do-gooding didn't exactly seem like it was making its way back to her yet.

She closed the door dejectedly. Then she kicked it, hard enough to leave a dent with her steel-toed combat boots. Things were so up in the air and uncertain these days. Chloe was still gone. Amy cursed herself for not hearing the phone when she'd called; it had been jammed at the bottom of her backpack and she had been outside, looking for Chloe, of all people. Amy started checking her voice mail about a thousand times an hour, hoping to hear something from her friend, but nothing.

She was definitely worried about Chloe. No doubt about it.

But she also felt a little . . . left behind. It was like she had made the decision to go out with Paul and now all these strange and mysterious things were going on in Chloe's life that Amy *still* wasn't in on. . . .

Alyec's famous barking laugh echoed down the hall. Amy looked: he was slamming his locker closed and waving goodbye to his friends Keira and Halley—very non-Chloe friends—and balancing his flute case on top of his notebook. *Off for a music lesson.*

Amy realized this was her perfect opportunity to thoroughly interrogate the untrustworthy jerk. She snuck along twenty feet behind him, keeping her back to the lockers, Harriet the Spy style. She needn't have bothered, though: Alyec was too busy waving to people in the main corridor to notice her.

As soon as he turned down toward the music wing, Amy double-timed her tiptoeing until she was almost four feet behind him. She didn't have to do it *too* quickly, though: he was dragging one of his legs a little. *What is that, some kind of new cool-guy walk?*

She smoothed her big dark red hair back and put on her best frowny face. She wished she could do the cold-blue-eyed thing—she had the eyes for it, after all—but somewhere between her freckles and "aristocratic" nose, she tended to come across more goofy and pleasant than aloof.

"You could just, I don't know, talk to me like a normal person," Alyec said causally, without looking behind him.

After she got over her surprise, Amy was so angry at being caught out she almost stamped her foot.

"*Where's Chloe?!*" she demanded. "I swear to *God*, Alyec Ilychovich, if you fucking *hurt* her . . . !"

A couple of students toting big, cumbersome instrument cases turned the corner, giggling and holding sheet music.

Alyec easily scooped an arm around Amy and pulled her into an empty practice room. He put his hand over her mouth and held a finger to his own. They stood there, his ice blue eyes locked on her own blue ones, insisting that she stay quiet until the two other students had passed.

31

He watched out the door to see if anyone else was coming and then took his hand away from her mouth.

"If you're not going to talk to me normally," Alyec said with a faint smile, "at least don't go throwing a psycho fit about it in public."

The room was mostly dark, on an inside wing with no windows. It was small and cluttered with the sort of desks and chairs small groups of students would sit in while practicing. In just a few minutes some teacher would come in and flip on the lights and the next period would begin. But for now it was just the two of them, and they were very alone. Alyec's chiseled-perfect face was inches from Amy's.

"You . . . *jerk!*" Amy lifted up her foot to stamp on his toes. He very neatly spun her away so she was at arm's length.

"She is home sick today, that is all," he said patiently.

That was what all the teachers had said when Amy had asked them, too.

"I *know* she said she was safe, but I *saw* what happened on the bridge," Amy said, sticking out her chin.

Alyec's blue eyes widened, and for once he didn't have a comeback.

"What's all this about?" she demanded. "Why was someone trying to kill Chloe? Twice? You know. I *know* you know."

He opened his mouth, looking for something to say. "She really is just sick at home. With her mother," he repeated lamely.

There was a long, tense moment between them, Amy glaring at him, *daring* him to lie again. He finally looked away.

Amy slammed her fist up into his stomach.

"*Jerk!*" she said again, stamping out into the hallway as he leaned over, hand to his belly. She knew she couldn't have done any real damage with her small wrists and the "artist's hands" that Chloe always made fun of, but at least he looked surprised. Amy spun around.

"Chloe is my best. Friend. *Ever,*" she hissed. "If any thing happens to her because of you, I'm getting my cousin Steve to beat the living *shit* out of you—and anyone else you know!"

She turned and left, adrenaline—if not exactly triumph—ringing in her ears.

Four

Chloe was snoozing, *The History of the Mai* resting on her lap, its old leather cover making her sneeze occasionally in her sleep. This was her second time trying to get through the dense text since she'd arrived, and the second time it had put her promptly to sleep.

She was dreaming again. This time a cat as large as a person walked toward her quietly. Chloe waited for it to tell her something useful or do something. . . .

"Am I disturbing you?" it said.

Chloe jumped, finally awake. She was *not* dreaming. The weird and ghostly visage that had terrified her the night before was standing patiently before her. *That's just Kim; she's a freak,* Alyec had said.

And boy, was he right.

She was a skinny and oddly built girl, willowy and sleek. Her hair was shorter than Chloe's, shiny, full, and black—almost blue-black, almost Asian. She had high cheekbones.

And velvety black cat ears.

Big ones. The size they would be if a cat's head were blown up to human proportions.

Her eyes were an unreal green, slit like a cat's, completely alien and lacking the appearance of normal human emotion. She wore a normal black tunic-length sweater and black jeans. She was barefoot; her bony toes had claws at the end and little tufts of black fur. Chloe couldn't help thinking about hobbits, except the girl was drop-dead gorgeous. She seemed about Chloe's age, but it was hard to tell.

"Uh, no, I was supposed to be reading anyway," Chloe said, running a hand over her face, trying not to stare.

"I'm afraid I gave you a bit of a scare when you arrived. I'm sorry—I do not usually expect, new, ah, people to be wandering around late at night."

"Hey, uh, no problem. My bad." Chloe kept on trying to look elsewhere, not sure what to say, still trying not to stare.

"I am—"

"Kim, yeah, Alyec told me."

The other girl looked annoyed. "My name is *Kemet* or Kem, *not* Kim. No one calls me that, though, thanks to people like Alyec." She sighed, sinking gracefully into the chair next to Chloe. "*Kemet* means 'Egypt.' Where we are from originally, thousands of years ago."

Chloe made a note to ask her about that later, but something else intrigued her more.

"Is that your given name?"

"No." Kim stared at the floor. "My given name is Greska."

"Oh." Chloe tried not to smile.

"You can see why I wanted to change it."

"Absolutely."

There was a moment of silence. Kim was looking into Chloe's face as curiously as Chloe was trying to avoid staring at the other girl.

"So we're from Egypt originally?" Chloe asked, trying to break Kim's icy, blinkless gaze. She closed the book. "I . . . uh . . . hadn't even gotten that far."

"We're first recorded, or history first mentions us there: 'Beloved of Bastet and guarded by Sekhmet.'" Kim took the book up and flipped to a page with a map on it and an inscription in hieroglyphs. "We were created by her, according to legend."

Chloe didn't know where to begin with her questions—*Created by? Ancient legends? Kim is my age and she can read ancient Egyptian writing?*

"Most of us in this pride are from Eastern Europe—"

"Wait, 'pride'?"

"Yes." The girl looked up at her coolly. If she'd had a tail, it would have been thumping impatiently. "That is the congregation our people travel in. Like lions."

"And Sergei is the leader of the . . . Pride?"

"No, just this one in California. There are four in the New World. Well, were. The one in the East is also primarily

37

made up of Eastern European Mai." Kim flipped a few pages and showed another map with statistics and inscriptions, lines and arrows originating from Africa and pointing toward different places: migration routes to lower Africa, Europe, and farther east. "The pride in New Orleans tends to be made up of Mai who stayed in sub-Saharan Africa the longest. They like the heat," she added with a disapproving twitch of her nose.

"And the fourth one?"

"It was . . . lost," Kim said diffidently. "Anyway, we have been driven all over the world, away from our homes. Our pride managed to live in Abkhazia for several hundred years after we left the Middle East for good." She pointed to a little area shaded pink to the northwest of Russia, on the Black Sea. "The people there remained polytheistic long after the Roman Empire declined, Christianity swept the world, and Baghdad was destroyed by the Mongols."

"I get the feeling that there's a 'but' in here somewhere. . . ."

"Many Abkhazians were driven out in the middle of the nineteenth century to Turkey by domestic warfare with the Georgians. We got caught up in it and families separated, some staying, some fleeing, some going to the Ukraine or St. Petersburg. And then again, not so long ago, just when some started to move back and reunite with lost branches, there was new violence."

She put the book down and twitched her nose

again—more like a rabbit than a cat, Chloe decided. It seemed to signal a change in emotion.

"I'm an orphan, just like you," the girl continued bluntly. "My parents were killed or separated during the Georgian-inspired violence in 1988, before the Wall fell. They say I had . . . a sister . . . ," she said slowly, looking at Chloe with hope. "A year older than me. When I saw you come in, I thought we looked alike— and . . . maybe . . ."

Maybe a little, except for the ears, was Chloe's first, defensive reaction. If you took away the ears, they actually *did* look a little similar: dark hair, fair skin, light eyes, high cheekbones.

What if it were true? Chloe had *always* wanted a sibling, especially a sister; Amy was the closest she had, but it still wasn't quite the same, like someone you could whisper to in the middle of the night or talk about your crazy parents with. Someone who you could scream at when she borrowed your favorite piece of clothing without telling you and then brought it back reeking of cigarette smoke or just plain ruined.

Someone who could tell you it was okay when you suddenly grew claws.

So maybe she's a little freaky, but a sister is a sister. . . .

"There wasn't any mention of siblings when my parents adopted me," Chloe said gently. "My parents told me they asked—they kind of wanted siblings to raise together."

"Ah, Slavic bureaucracy. Who knows what they recorded and what they didn't?"

"They never said anything about a place called Abkhazia either. . . ."

"The issues surrounding it and the country itself are not commonly known to Western . . . ah . . . normal people."

"Well, I've always wanted a sister," Chloe said softly, hoping to cheer up the other girl.

"I have been looking for years." Kim sighed. "Sergei has a whole department dedicated to trying to track down all of our relatives: parents, family trees, missing cousins. . . . We even send things out for genetic testing to establish relationships."

"Wow. That's impressive." Actually it sounded a little nuts, like a more proactive version of Amy's grandmother and her family tree obsession.

"It's *survival*, Chloe," Kim said, fixing Chloe's eyes with her own. "There are very few of us left."

Both of them were silent for a moment.

"Ah, Chloe!" Sergei came bounding in, arms outstretched as if he was going to hug her again. She shrank reflexively back, not from distaste but fear of being squeezed to death. "My meetings are over, and it is time for lunch." He stopped short of actually hugging her, giving a casual, uninterested nod toward Kim. "I thought you could join me. We'll get some nice salads or whatever you young kids eat today. And I can show you what we do here."

"Sure, if you don't mind. . . ." She turned, but Kim was already silently padding out of the room, again, like Olga, backing away, facing Sergei until the last minute before turning.

"Also, I told Valerie and Olga to scare you up some clothes. What are you, size eight?"

Chloe jumped. A brief worry that he might not be taking care of her in a strictly fatherly fashion must have flashed over her face.

Sergei chuckled. "My family were leatherworkers, Chloe. In Sukhumi. I grew up among vests and coats and saddles and knowing how to fit a customer." Sergei put his arm around her shoulders and began to lead her out.

"Uh, can I ask one question? If it's not rude?" she ventured.

"Anything, Chloe."

"Why does Kim—I mean, do we all . . . I mean . . . the ears?" She made a motion with her finger.

Sergei rolled his eyes. "Kim is a very religious person. She is following a particular path to bring her closer to the Goddesses. In her beliefs, it is what we all looked like a long time ago."

"She . . . *wants* to look that way?"

"Something like that. She's a very intelligent and pious girl, but kind of . . . zealous." The older man said it in the exact same tone Alyec had said "a freak."

"Do you worship—?" She wanted to say "the Goddesses," "ancient Egyptian gods," or some such, but

41

it was hard while they passed copy machines and short-sleeved cubicle slaves at messy, piled desks.

"It is hard for anyone who grew up in the shadow of the Communist Soviet Union to really worship anything," he said gently. "I follow Sekhmet as best as I can. Olga was raised sort of Russian Orthodox, with some worship of Bastet, too."

They stopped in an office of slightly calmer people with bigger desks. Chloe recognized Igor, shouting in Russian on a phone. Standing next to him was an assistant, a boy about Brian's age, with trendy thick glasses and a look of resigned hopelessness.

"Is everyone here . . . Mai?" Chloe whispered.

"To the last one. I built up this little real estate empire so everyone could have a place to work with their own people if they chose."

"Does everyone . . . in the pride . . . work here?"

Sergei shook his head. "Valerie, Igor's fiancée, is a model. Simone is a dancer. And Kim does her own thing, as they say. But it's difficult for us to hold down corporate jobs—people can sniff out the wolves among the sheep, or the cats among the . . . well, you know. We don't fit in."

Chloe looked at Igor. He seemed like a normal overworked human male. His tie was thrown over his shoulder and his shoes were trendy. He took notes with a pencil and played with a desk toy as he spoke. But the way he arched his back, and the way the light hit his

42

brown eyes and made them glow for a moment, and the way he swung his head to look at Sergei and Chloe and didn't blink—taken all together, there was indeed something very different about him.

Igor put one hand over the receiver and held out the other when he saw Chloe and Sergei standing there.

"Hello," he said in an accent that was noticeably Russian. *Or noticeably something.*

"I'm Chloe." She felt something strange poke her on her skin as she shook his hand— and realized that his claws had come out and were gently pricking her. *A secret greeting,* she realized, trying to do it back. She pressed too hard, though, underestimating her strength. Igor pulled back his hand, grinning ruefully, and sucked on the pad of his palm where she had drawn blood.

"I've never done that before," Chloe said, blushing. "The handshake thing."

Sergei thought it was hysterical.

"That's my girl. A man-eater!" He slapped her so hard on the back, she almost pitched into Igor's lap. But he was already shouting back into the phone.

"Igor is my right-hand man. I'd be helpless without him," Sergei confided. Somehow, Chloe didn't believe that. "Right now he's working on an old, uh, massage parlor near Union Square. We plan to put franchises in it, like Starbucks. Maybe a Quiznos."

"That's terrible," Chloe said before she could stop herself. "I mean, that must be very profitable." She paused. "But I mean, it might have a bad history, but at least the place has, you know, an interesting one. Not a strip-mall-y one."

"Ah, you're one of those." Sergei sighed. "If it's any consolation, we just worked with the city to turn the space next to a vacant lot into a city-subsidized child-care center for low-income women and the lot into a community garden for them."

"Hell of a tax break," Igor whispered, holding his hand over the receiver again.

Sergei frowned at him, and the boy went meekly back to work.

"At least consider a bookstore," Chloe pleaded. "Even a Barnes & Noble."

"Look at this, I have my own little spiritual adviser." Sergei fluffed the hair on her head. "Maybe we'll put you to work while you're not in school—like an intern. Then you can make your voice heard. Heh. Come, let's order lunch." He whirled his arm around Chloe's shoulders, and dragged her with him.

Five

"The emergency meeting of the Order will now come to session."

It was a lot less formal than most of the meetings Brian was forced to attend: in daylight, no less, and in normal street clothes. *Well, street clothes for me. Suits for all of these old—*

"Purpose?" his father asked ritually, for the stenographer to take down. Brian watched in disgust as his dad, Whitney Rezza, flexed his fingers, admiring the ancient gold ring and his own manicured fingernails. Metrosexuals had nothing on *his* dad. He'd practically invented the style.

"To determine once and for all what to do about Chloe King," said The Nonce. The Nonce was Edna Hilohire in real life and a dead ringer for Dame Judith Anderson. Her age, short hair, dry wit, and sharp, piggy little brown eyes all made her seem as powerful as she was—so were most of the inner circle of the Order.

Rich, white, and mostly middle-aged. Brian's grandfather, the venerable Elder of this Conclave, was *ancient*. He at least seemed to understand Brian's hesitation to go along with the group about Chloe, if not forgive it. *Or permit it, more importantly,* thought Brian.

"Directly or indirectly, she is responsible for the Rogue's death." This was said by weaselly Richard, the little yes-man Brian's dad loved to keep around. Richard—Dick—might be Whit Rezza's favorite, but almost everyone else referred to him as Dick*less*. He was doing all he could to become leader someday. It was a position that Brian had once hoped for and had almost been guaranteed, due to his lineage, but then things had changed. *Everything* had changed when he met Chloe.

Brian had never chosen to be part of this world of Tenth Bladers, unlike Richard, who chose to join of his own free will. There was something about secrecy, rituals, devotion, and danger that seemed to draw people in at every age, Brian reflected bitterly.

Brian never would have chosen this life for himself. If he'd ever had any choice, that is. That was how he'd somehow wound up at a committee meeting determining the fate of the only girl he'd ever felt strongly about. Maybe even loved.

"She is *not* directly—or even *in*directly responsible for his death," Brian repeated tiredly for the thousandth time since that night, when he had returned home from the fight on the bridge. He ran his hand through his dark brown hair, normally full, now lank with exhaustion and sweat. "Alexander Smith came to *kill* her, and she defended herself. What's more, when he slipped off the bridge *by his own actions*, she put out a hand to *save* him."

"I find that highly unlikely," Richard said primly.

"Shut up," Brian snapped at him. "You weren't even there."

"Easy, Novitiate," Edna said. "You are almost out of line." But she said it with a faint smile. "While I, too, find it hard to believe that *anyone*, Mai or human, would try to help someone who just tried to kill her, the only witness we have at present is Brian."

"Whose views are obviously prejudiced," his father stated in the rich, stirring tones of a leader. "Let it be noted that I will not allow love for my own son to interfere with the facts of the proceedings."

Like it's ever interfered before, thought Brian.

"There is no proof of the Rogue's death," Ramone, the minute-taker, offered. He was a tall, gaunt young man, every inch the Librarian he was supposed to be—except for his healthy skin tone and fairly radiant brown eyes. He wasn't much older than Brian but already sounded ancient. "I have gone through police and hospital records. No bodies have washed ashore, or been trawled, or—"

"That means nothing," Brian's father said again. "He fell. Defending himself."

47

"From a girl who was defending *her*self!" Brian protested.

"Strike that last statement," Mr. Rezza ordered Ramone. "It is of no consequence and out of order."

"You know, it was *you* people who first put me onto her case," Brian said angrily.

"Yes, and we expected you to follow, befriend, and observe the Mai in question. We did not ask you to become her advocate!"

"Let us turn to the mother," Edna interrupted politely, clasping her hands on the table. She too wore a ring of the Order, but it was smaller, in an orange gold that was different than that of Brian's dad's. "Is she safe?"

"For now." Brian didn't miss the look his dad gave Edna: *We'll discuss it later,* it said.

"Well, that is one thing we can be grateful for." The old woman leaned forward, spreading her hands. "Let us continue tracking Chloe, much more closely this time, using someone, ah . . ." She glanced in apology to Brian. "Not *directly* involved with her heretofore. As long as we know where she is, we can make our decision at any time, and meanwhile, we can watch to see if she does anything else violent."

"That seems reasonable," Ramone said.

"All right," Brian's dad said. "Agreed. Brian, you are off the case. *Really.* If you are caught anywhere near Chloe King again—there will be consequences."

48

*Like what? You'll dock my allowance? You'll ground me?
You'll somehow let Mom get killed* again? Brian's dark
brown eyes burned with a rusty fire deep within. His
father had punished him enough already for an entire
lifetime. He couldn't possibly do any more.

"Where was she last seen?"

"Running away from the bridge. The National
Guard was alerted to the Rogue's presence by her
friends," Brian mumbled.

"Her *human* friends," Edna said. Brian nodded.

"She wound up on the Marin Headlands, but I lost
her there."

"Was anyone else with her?"

His father looked him straight in the eye. His were a
rheumy old blue like a dark sky with clouds; Brian had
gotten most of his looks from his mom.

Brian thought about Alyec, the drop-dead gorgeous
"other" boyfriend of Chloe's, the high-school student,
another Mai. One who could touch and kiss Chloe and
not die from doing it, unlike Brian.

His nemesis.

"No," he said slowly. "She was completely alone."

Six

"Take these over to Misha," the feral receptionist flatly ordered Chloe, dropping a stack of contracts into her arms.

Chloe sighed and began the task of trying to find yet another hidden office in the archaic complex that was Firebird. It was strange to go from a halogen-lit bright copy room with faxes, computers, copiers, and phones, for instance, to a tiny bathroom with a pull-chain toilet and a steam radiator that took up half the room.

Sergei had followed up his own suggestion that she intern a bit around the office to alleviate boredom and was paying her a fairly decent ten bucks an hour. Fine, she couldn't actually go out and spend anywhere, but the thought was nice. And she was learning a lot about the business of real estate, most importantly that this was one thing she definitely did *not* want to do when she grew up.

She knocked on a door she thought was Misha's, one

of the in-house paralegals, but instead walked in on Igor and his gorgeous blond fiancée, Valerie, staring at each other starry-eyed on a couch.

"Uh, sorry," Chloe muttered, hastily closing the door. She was looking up and down the hallway again, trying to figure out where she was, when her cell phone rang. She had accidentally left it on after checking her voice mail, listening to *more* messages from Amy. *Well, at least she's properly worried. Teaches her for ditching me for so long,* Chloe couldn't help thinking.

She looked at the caller ID and sucked in her breath.

"Hello?" she asked quietly. No one had said anything explicitly against her using the cell phone, but somehow she suspected they wouldn't be particularly thrilled about the idea, either.

"Chloe? It's Brian."

From his voice it was obvious he didn't know what to expect; he sounded hesitant but urgent. The scene at the Marin Headlands flashed through her mind again: running with Alyec, Alyec falling, a throwing star sticking out of his leg. Above the two of them Brian, with another throwing star in his hand.

"What do you want?"

There was a long pause; she heard him swallowing, could picture his brooding, handsome face as he tried to come up with the right thing to say. She could practically see him frowning a little, his brow knitting over his dark, bottomless eyes.

"Are you okay?" he finally asked.

"I'm fine. I'm with some people who are protecting me."

"You . . . found the Pride, then."

She shouldn't have been surprised by his deduction; who else would it be? The police? The federal witness protection program, as Sergei had told her mom?

"Yes," she answered evenly. "And they're going to try to find out who my parents are, too. What happened to my biological family." *Why am I telling him this stuff? Why do I still want him to know about my life? About me?*

"Oh." There was another pause. Chloe was a little disappointed, but after all, he couldn't really say, "That's nice," or "Good for you," when the people involved were outright enemies of his organization. Whatever his personal beliefs were, the group he belonged to had only one intention: to wipe out the Mai or keep them under control. It was still hard for Chloe to understand.

"Chloe, I really was trying to help you on the bridge."

"Really? By almost cutting Alyec's hamstring in half?"

"I told you," he said impatiently. "If you two had kept running that way, you would have wound up right in the middle of an outpost. And believe me, there may not be many members as psychotic as the Rogue, but there are more than enough members of the Tenth Blade who wouldn't think *twice* about taking down a pair of Mai. Especially one that was somehow involved in the death of the Rogue."

"I didn't . . ." But she trailed off when she realized

what he'd actually said. He hadn't said that she had killed him. He hadn't even said that she was responsible for his death. "Well, you had no trouble targeting Alyec. Why weren't you able to get the Rogue in the throat?"

"Chloe," he said a little pleadingly, a little sadly. "Do you think it's easy to just *kill* another person? Even if they're doing something awful? Especially if he's a . . . friend of the family?"

Chloe didn't want to listen to this. He should have just wanted to save her and not given a thought to anything else. *That was* what she wanted—or at least that was what she wanted to hear.

"Even *you* weren't ready to let him die," he said quietly. "I saw you give him your hand."

He had a good point. Why had she tried to help save her own assassin? *Because it seemed like the right thing to do.* So why did she blame Brian for not automatically coming to her aid and killing for her?

"I have never killed anyone," he added. "Not human, not Mai, not anyone. And I don't want to start."

"You could have done something," Chloe muttered, feeling childish and not knowing why.

"It looked like you were doing a pretty good job yourself."

She could hear the smile in his voice, beyond the sadness. For just an instant, she wished she could see him. She could just imagine him reaching over and stroking her cheek at that point or touching her hand. . . .

And suddenly she realized something.

"I know why you didn't want to kiss me," she said slowly, not caring that it had nothing to do with what they were just talking about. She remembered her conversation with Sergei that morning and with Alyec, days ago, when he'd first seen her with Brian.

"You haven't done anything with him." It was a statement, not a question.

"Yeah? How would you know?"

"He's still alive." Alyec grinned at her. *"You would tear a boy like that up and spit him back out when you were done."*

He had been deadly serious, not speaking metaphorically at all. She thought about what had happened to Xavier and the time Brian had almost thrown her away from him when she was trying to steal a kiss.

No wonder Alyec wasn't jealous of Brian! He knew there was no future in it.

"I'm sorry. I really did want to. I mean . . ." He paused. "I do."

"Was it all an act?" she whispered. "Just so you could keep an eye on me?"

"No, Chloe, I swear it wasn't," he said desperately. "I didn't mean to fall in love with you."

And there it was, hanging in the air. He sort of choked out the last bit quickly, at the end, as if he hadn't meant to say it, as if it had just come out of nowhere.

Chloe opened her mouth to say something, but no

sound came. Her ears twitched; familiar footsteps came stomping down the hall.

"I have to go," she said.

"I—" He seemed to know that now was not the time to push. "I'll talk to you later. Be careful, okay? You're a . . . wanted woman these days."

Chloe smiled at the double entendre.

"I will."

She flipped the phone closed just as Alyec barged into the room.

"Chloe! Love of my life!" he cried, flinging his arms open dramatically. Chloe flinched; this was a poor time for him to be throwing words like that around.

"Hey, who were you talking to? Paul? Amy?"

Hearing their names come out of his mouth was strange. Their weird double date a couple of weeks ago aside, the four of them had never really hung out. They weren't two couples, or four friends, or anything like that. Paul had the comics thing with Alyec, but Amy absolutely hated him. Chloe wondered if he even knew how she felt about him.

As Alyec put his notebook and books down on a chair, Chloe couldn't help staring at his perfect body. Not too muscled, but broad shouldered and well defined. It was like he might fall into a fashion magazine without even realizing it. Alyec was probably the hottest guy in her school. But Alyec's bodily perfection so soon after a talk with Brian was only distracting and even a little upsetting.

He noticed her mood immediately.

"Talking to a secret *lover*, maybe?" he asked, grinning. He cocked his head knowingly at her, coming close as if to take her in for a kiss. Then he grabbed the phone from her.

"Hey!" she shouted. "Give it!"

He laughed and danced around her, holding it high above his head, at least two feet out of her reach. She jumped and leapt in a completely human fashion, pulling at his arms and forgetting all of the cat training he had led her through on that mysterious night when Chloe first learned what she could do as a Mai.

"Let's find out who you were calling . . . if you have another boyfriend. . . ." Just as he flipped it open and started hitting the menu keys, Chloe made one last desperate leap to stop him. The phone was almost in her grasp. . . .

"Hey! Catch!" he shouted suddenly to Igor and Valerie, who were walking by. As Alyec tossed the phone, Igor reached out and caught it gracefully. *Catlike reflexes,* Chloe thought. He and Valerie smiled at the other couple. Chloe ran at them. Igor spun and tossed the phone back to Alyec seconds before Chloe reached him. Valerie laughed and they walked on.

"Give it," Chloe growled, beginning to lose her temper.

Alyec responded by flipping open her phone and looking through the incoming calls list. He danced away as she frantically tried to throw herself against him. But when he saw Brian's name, he hesitated. Then he closed the phone and handed it back to Chloe, trying to maintain a cheerful, playful look on his face. But Chloe hadn't missed the moment of hurt.

"I wasn't telling him where I was or where your secret base camp is," she said defensively.

"I didn't think you did," he said, a little sadly. Silence hung between them for a moment. "I'm hungry. Let's go see what's around," he said, trying to muster up a little bravado. He picked up his books again. "You really *should* call Paul and Amy," he added quietly. "They're worried about you."

There it was again, those two names out of his mouth. Like he really was a close member of her life now, someone who had met her mom, taken her out on dates, and fed her chocolate during her period, and not someone she had done everything to keep her mom from meeting, who had taught her how to extend her claws, to climb trees, and run on rooftops at night.

Chloe put the phone in her back pocket and followed him out of the room.

Seven

Paul was happy just staring at Amy.

They were at Café Eland, and his girlfriend was animatedly talking about her day. He never really got over how she *sparkled*. Chloe was pretty, too, but different. Sort of reserved, held closely inward. Though she would be the last to admit it, Chloe King was an introspective person, prone to occasional insight and moody sulks, which was why her semi-disappearance from his and Amy's life—before her *real* disappearance three days ago—didn't surprise or upset him as much as it did Amy.

But with Amy, what you saw was what you got. If she was feeling something, no matter what it was, you knew it immediately. There was no guessing her moods or mind games. And even if some of her ideas and leanings were passing beyond the border of eccentric and well into the country of the insane, at least she had amazing amounts of energy to put into it.

Her dark red hair—almost back to its natural color,

Paul noted—was framing her face and bouncing gently as she waved her hands around and spoke excitedly. He looked deep into her beautiful marble blue eyes, smiling, his harelip scar barely tugging his skin.

"And *then* he put his hand over my mouth and dragged me into the room!"

She said this so loudly that not only did Paul come to, but half of the café stopped for a moment to listen.

"Wait, what?" He shook his head. He knew he should have been listening, but Amy talked a *lot*. All the time, in fact. He couldn't help tuning out once in a while.

"Alyec!" she repeated with exasperation. "When I told him that he had better not have hurt Chloe. He *grabbed* me and dragged me into the music theory room."

"Why did you do that? Why *would* you do that?"

"Blame the victim, why don't you?" Amy huffed. "Typical male."

Even though he was confused and impatient to find out exactly what had happened, Paul thought over his next words carefully. "Did he hurt you?"

"No," Amy admitted grudgingly. "But he grabbed my arm and put his hand over my mouth!"

"Did he threaten you?"

"Yes!"

Paul waited, staring steadily at her with his dark brown eyes, raising one of his perfectly rectangular eyebrows.

"No," Amy finally said under his scrutiny, looking down at her coffee and kicking the table leg like a little girl. "But he *might* have. If there hadn't been other people nearby."

"So wait—you accused him of doing something to Chloe in the hall in front of other people?"

"No, I'm not an *idiot*. There were just some band geeks walking by."

Paul sat back and stirred his tea slowly, not wanting to look her in the face while he digested everything. Paul could be enigmatic, but sometimes he was just so stunned by what Amy said or did that it took a moment for him to adjust.

"But he knows *something* about what's going on," Amy said desperately, unable to bear his silence. "When I told him what we saw on the bridge, he got all surprised and weird and stuff."

Paul reached for the zipper under his neck and loosened it a little, playing with the tag as if it were a tie. It was his new Puma running jacket, sleek, with red stripes going down the sides. When he wore it, he fit in perfectly with the older, "real" DJs at the clubs he liked. It was like his personal superhero costume.

"Amy," he finally said, "you shouldn't have done that. If he's innocent—and let me remind you that you still don't have any real proof of anything—then it was crazy and mean. And if he *is* involved somehow, how is confronting him like that going to help?"

Amy frowned. "I told him if he hurt Chloe, I would kill him."

Paul tried not to smile. "Very John Constantine of you."

"You're a *jerk*," Amy said, so distracted she sucked hot coffee up through the stirrer. She tried not to react, maintaining her dignity. Paul sighed inwardly, knowing he would just have to wait it out. *We have time for what, one, maybe two more mood swings tonight?* While it occurred to him that this was a little tiresome sometimes, he wasn't sure he'd have it any other way. For now he would stay. They would talk. And later they would make up.

Eight

Chloe and Alyec had Firebird's lounge to themselves that night. Sergei had made it very clear that there were to be no boys anywhere near Chloe's bedroom, and she knew that meant Alyec especially. So the lounge was as private as they could get.

The lights were dimmed, candles were lit, and she and Alyec were lying on the floor, eating some post-make-out Chinese.

"It's better than going to a restaurant," Alyec said, delicately stuffing his face with lo mein. His skill with chopsticks was extraordinary. "No one else is here, and we can do whatever we want."

Chloe was clumsier with her own set of chopsticks and had to resort to tipping the mostly empty carton of fried rice into her mouth while digging at the bottom with a single stick, making it fall in great clumps into her mouth.

He sucked up a last noodle as lasciviously as he

could without getting soy sauce all over everything. Then he leaned forward and kissed her, briefly licking her teeth with the tip of his salty tongue.

She rolled over to him and kissed him more, holding the back of his head so he couldn't pull away. He didn't try. He mouthed his way off her lips and down to her neck; as he traced the delicate veins on her skin there, she felt her claws extend. She threw her head back, enjoying it.

"Chloe," he whispered, pulling back and smiling gently at her. "I have to go."

"Tease!" she said, only half pretending to be upset. She felt her claws retract again.

"Mom's giving me a ride home," he said apologetically. "I should go find her unless you want to keep making out and have her walk in on us. . . ."

"No, I understand." Chloe sat up, sighing. "It's just that I don't really get to see you anymore. Now that I don't go to school—I mean, I used to see you at least off and on all day."

"I know," he said, kissing her on the forehead. "It was one of the few reasons I looked forward to going."

"How long were you interested in me? I mean, before we really talked?" Chloe asked, her face brightening.

"A *long* time before I knew you were Mai."

"If I was human, what would you have done?"

"The same thing I did with Keira Hendelson. *And* Halley Dietrich. Nothing. Not that I wanted to!" he added quickly when she raised her hand to hit him.

Chloe backed down and began to pick at the fried rice again, trying to make the two chopsticks work. "Do you hate humans? The way Sergei seems to?"

Alyec shrugged. "It's hard to hate six billion people all at once. Sometimes it is difficult being in both worlds. Like . . ." He shifted position as he really thought about it. Chloe tried to remain as casual and silent as she could; this was the most he had ever really talked about his feelings. "Like I'll be listening to music or whatever at my locker, slapping hands with someone, and that will all be fine but at night, you know, when the sun sets, I get that urge to *run*, explore the night, chase after something. For a while I can be tricked into thinking I am completely human, but there is no denying that other, completely different world we inhabit."

"Why aren't you in danger going to school like this? By yourself? Won't the Tenth Blade try to kill you?"

Alyec shook his head and stuffed another dumpling into his mouth, the moment of reflection over.

"We're at kind of a stalemate. If they out-and-out killed *me*, it would mean instant retribution from the Mai. War. Newbies, prideless Mai, don't count—like you before we got you. Because technically you are not under any protection. In this 'modern' world, the Tenth Blade doesn't tend to attack members of a pride unless they hurt or kill a human."

"It all seems a little . . ." Chloe looked for a word, thinking of *The Godfather*. "*Archaic.*"

Alyec shrugged. "How is this fantastic bedroom of yours I'm not allowed to see?"

He wasn't changing the subject because it made him uncomfortable; he was really just done with it and moving on to other things.

"Oh, it's pretty cool. Usually after everyone's gone to sleep, all the girls come over in their skimpy jammies and we have pillow fights until we're all basically naked."

Alyec's eyes lit up for a moment, and then his face fell. "You're lying," he realized.

"You think?" She popped another dumpling into her mouth. It was scallion and vegetable, and she was secretly relieved she still liked that kind. Chloe had been experiencing a quiet but growing fear that she would become a complete carnivore the more time she spent with the Mai. "Sergei wanted to give me a real room, like with a four-poster bed and all this wonderful stuff, but I asked to stay in the first room. You know, the little gable they let me nap in. I love it. Everything is sort of dusty pink and green. It's the bedroom I've always dreamed of," she said shyly. "Kind of like living in my own version of a Gothic novel."

"Like *The Scarlet Letter*?"

It was what they had been reading in English when Chloe was forced to disappear. She felt a brief pang of sadness as she thought of Mr. Mingrone sketching little *A*'s on the blackboard.

"No, more like, I don't know, *Wuthering Heights* or something."

"Oh. I think we have to read that next year." He gathered up his garbage neatly and stuffed it into one of the plastic bags the delivery came in, making sure to put lids back on the little dishes of soy sauce so they wouldn't spill. Chloe watched him, amused. When he was through, Alyec leaned over and kissed her gently on the lips. "Goodbye, Chloe King. I'll see you the evening after tomorrow?"

"What's tomorrow? A prom committee meeting?"

"As a matter of fact, yes." He winked and kissed her again. He squeezed her hand and left.

Chloe sighed, watching him go, then began to blow out all the candles. Her evening of romance—her couple of hours of normalcy—were over. She gathered up the bags of garbage and went in search of the kitchenette to throw them out. For a moment she happily imagined that this was what college life would be like: a hard day of classes, a cheap date in the dorm's common room, and then borrowing incense from a next-door stoner to refresh the place after complaints from vegan neighbors.

Chloe wondered if she would ever get to college at this rate. How was she going to make up for the time lost in school? Maybe they had a copy of *The Scarlet Letter* in the library somewhere. Maybe she could home-school herself. Apparently Kim did.

She started to open a door in a nearby hall, thinking

it was the kitchenette, but stopped cold when she realized what she was looking at. The room was large and mostly dark, lit by candles and oil lamps. The floor was made up of thick tiles of rough-hewn sandy stone, and in the back was sort of a stage, set higher than the floor. On this stage were two huge statues like the bookends she had seen in the library. The left one was a human with a lioness's head. On the right sat a giant black Egyptian stone cat, an earring in her right ear and a smile on her kitty lips. Separating the stage from the rest of the room was what could only be described as a moat, a thin rectangle of water stretching the width of the room.

Kim was kneeling at a little altar in front of those statues, her head down. She wore a rough, off-white robe and was murmuring quietly. Except for the three-dimensional perspective, it could have been a painting off an ancient Egyptian wall.

Chloe tried not to make any noise but accidentally scuffed her sneaker against the lintel. Kim's black cat ears flicked back in response to the noise, although the rest of her didn't move.

"Sorry," Chloe whispered.

Kim seemed to finish whatever she was doing and stood up.

"Didn't mean to disturb you . . ."

"No problem," Kim said easily. She slipped out of the robe and hung it on a rack near the door, where similar robes were hung, in different sizes. Under it she wore her usual outfit: jeans, a sweater, no socks or shoes.

"What's, uh, what's all that about?" Chloe asked as casually as she could, jerking her thumb at the two statues, afraid of the answer she would get.

"Those are our gods, Bastet and Sekhmet," Kim said seriously. "Two forms of the same goddess."

"Does, uh . . . everybody . . . ?" She tried to imagine Alyec kneeling in a white robe to ancient, foreign statues and couldn't.

"Not to the extent that I do."

Kim's ears twitched occasionally toward various noises in different rooms.

Chloe had to ask the question. *Well, I am a cat, after all, and curiosity hasn't killed me yet. . . .*

"Uh—I hope you don't mind me asking, but Sergei said you thought we all used to, uh, look like you, but how did you—?"

"I follow the path of the ancients," Kim responded, a little primly.

Chloe just raised her eyebrows and shook her head; it meant nothing to her.

"If you were to keep your claws out and your night vision constant for many years, you would look the same," the other girl responded, running a hand claw over one of her ears. "It takes a lot of concentration and meditation and prayer."

"O-kay." *Meditation? Prayer? What have I gotten myself into?*

69

Chloe's parents had never been particularly devout: her mother had been raised Episcopalian and her father Catholic, but they didn't take her to church on a regular basis. She had never really had to *think* about religion before, not apart from occasionally joining Amy for Passover or remembering to watch her mouth around Paul's more religious Baptist relatives. After her father left, Chloe's mom tried taking her to Anglican churches like she had gone to with her own more religious mother, but this was halfhearted and only lasted until Chloe put her foot down as a dissenting teenager.

Chloe focused back on the present and Kim, the weird girl before her with the cat aspect. What would her Episcopalian mother think now?

"I don't know if I can. . . ."

"Many have the same problem," Kim said soothingly. "They aren't accustomed to worshiping any god at all. But they are Mai and always choose a path. The way of Bastet is maternal love, the home, and physical, emotional, and spiritual nourishment." She pointed to the cat.

"Oh, like Olga?" Chloe remembered Sergei telling her. "How she takes care of everyone?"

Kim nodded. "Sekhmet is the side of war, disease, violence, protection." She pointed to the enthroned statue.

"Oh." Chloe thought uncomfortably of Sergei. "She's, uh . . . evil?"

"Neither goddess is *evil*," Kim said patiently. "They

just *are*. Sekhmet is the goddess of our soldiers, the kizekh, and she defends her young fiercely. Like a mother lion protects her cubs."

"Who else follows her? Besides Sergei and the 'kizekh,' I mean?" Chloe laughed uneasily, thinking of Alyec and unable to imagine him following either.

"That is a question you would do well to consider," Kim suggested. It would have sounded patronizing from anyone else, but with her alien, emotionless green eyes it sounded wise. "Before you make your own choice."

"Who do you follow?"

"Both. They are two sides of the same coin, a wholeness that is too often forgotten."

The lights in the room flickered. For just a moment it was as if a wind blew through the room, a zephyr from another, forgotten land. Chloe and Kim stood a few feet apart, and as their shadows seized and danced in the wavering light, Chloe noticed how frail the girl seemed, almost hollow. *An orphan, like me. Without even an adopted family.* No wonder she threw herself into these ancient rituals and history—it was a way of connecting herself with something, of fitting in with their people, even if it was only their past.

I may be a newcomer, but she's always been a loner.

"Huh. Hey, can you show me where the kitchen is? I got a little lost." Kim nodded and padded silently out before her, beckoning her to follow. "And can I ask you another question?"

"By all means."

"So there are very few of us left, we have these weird catlike characteristics, the Tenth Blade watches our every move. . . ."

Kim was nodding. She opened a door and Chloe filed after her into the small, linoleum-white room she had been looking for.

"Why don't the rich ones just pool resources and buy some frickin' huge tract of land somewhere—like, a hundred acres or whatever—and have everyone just move there and live happily ever after? Just a little independent Mai survivalist community where everyone can show their claws and hunt and use the litter pan or whatever?"

Kim ignored her last comment. "Some say it is our curse," she answered simply.

Chloe dumped the garbage in the can that was under the sink, then opened the fridge, looking for dessert. "What?"

"Our curse." In a fluid movement Kim leapt backward up onto the counter next to the sink and sat with her legs dangling down. It was one of the most human things Chloe had seen her do. "Five thousand years ago or so, the stories say that a Mai girl and human boy fell in love in the Upper Kingdom. *Egypt*," she added.

There was a lot of meat and cold cuts in the fridge. Good-looking stuff. Also weird pickled stuff, bottles and bottles of beets.

"Neither side was particularly thrilled with this, but

it wasn't unheard of—back then. One night, when the two lovers were supposed to meet, the girl, Neferet, was ambushed by friends of the boy's family and killed. Possibly raped and tortured," she added, almost as an afterthought. "In retaliation the Mai called upon their brethren and set out in the night, every night, until the moon was new again and disappeared from the sky, and killed *every human within a twenty-mile radius.*"

"Is this all true?"

Kim shrugged. "That is what is written. The gods cursed the Mai. Even Bastet and Sekhmet abandoned their own children. Never again would human and Mai be able to love, and the Mai would be driven from their homeland for thousands of years, unable to settle down until the wrong had been righted."

"And again I ask: Is this true?"

"It doesn't matter whether or not a thing is true if it is what people believe," Kim said philosophically. "Every time we seem to find a new home, something happens. Ugarit. Ur. Ashur. All destroyed, and we were forced to move on. The Diaspora from Abkhazia was only one of the latest examples. This particular pride used to have its headquarters in LA. Then our home was destroyed by the earthquake in '94. These *things* keep happening, to the point where even the skeptical become disheartened and draw the conclusion that we really aren't meant to live anywhere permanently until we have overcome our past."

Chloe was listening, but she also noticed an area of the fridge that was locked off, like a strongbox. She raised an eyebrow at Kim and pointed at it.

"It's where the adults keep the alcohol," she answered in the same even tone in which she had been telling the stories.

"I could really do with a beer," Chloe said wistfully.

"'Beer' in ancient Egyptian, as well as the old language of the Mai, is *henqet*," Kim said, a little pedantically. Then she raised her hand and extended her index finger, pointing her beautiful, thick black claw. She hopped off the counter and bent over to the fridge, inserting her claw into the lock. After fiddling with it for a moment, there was a *click* and the door swung open.

Inside were a bunch of frosty bottles of Rolling Rock as well as Michelob Ultras, Sam Adamses, and Anchor Steams.

Chloe took two out, offering one to Kim.

"To the Mai," she said, clinking a bottle.

"To Bastet and Sekhmet," Kim answered back, flipping the top off neatly with her thumb claw.

As Chloe downed the wheaty bubbles, she decided that she was beginning to really like this freaky girl.

Nine

On Wednesday, Paul was still thinking about what Amy had told him when he'd pulled his wallet out of his locker, ready to go across the street for comic day. Alyec had also been at his locker, down the hall. Paul had felt a wave of embarrassment, almost afraid that the other guy saw him. He had to do something about this.

As casually as he could, he strolled down the hallway toward the exit, past Alyec.

"Hey, Ruskie, you coming?" he called.

"Yeah, hang on." Alyec tossed his blond hair out of his face as he pulled his head out of the bottom of his locker, then slammed the door and joined Paul. "Did you read this month's *Wizard*? I think I might want to try *Heroes of the Adamantine Age*."

Paul shrugged. "I really like the writer, but I can't *stand* Dave Applebee's art. It's so out of proportion. All muscles and tits and calves, like it's still 1982 or something."

"It's *nostalgic*!"

They walked out of school in silence. Paul had to walk slowly: Chloe's boyfriend was favoring one leg. Halfway to the store Alyec gave Paul a sideways look.

"Your girlfriend's a complete psycho," he said without malice.

"I know." Paul sighed, relieved that the other boy had brought it up first. "I'm sorry about that."

"Not your fault. She has a pretty wild imagination, though."

He should let it go. He *knew* it. He should follow his own advice. But he had to ask.

"Is Chloe safe? Just tell me that," he said quietly.

Alyec rolled his eyes. "You *too*? Are both of you crazy conspiracy freaks or something?"

Paul stopped and ticked off points with his fingers. "Weird stuff *has* been going on with Chloe since, you know, *you* and Chloe. She was fighting for her life on Friday, and suddenly you develop a limp at the same time. And you're her *boyfriend*, and you don't seem that concerned that she's been 'out sick' for the last three days. In fact, you don't seem very worried at all. . . . Which leads me to believe that you know something about what's going on and that she's okay."

Alyec was quiet a long moment.

"You're smarter than your girlfriend, too," he finally said.

"Nah," Paul said, smiling. "She's the über-PSAT girl. I just think *longer* than she does."

Alyec bit his lip—*Like a girl,* Paul thought—and tapped his hands against his sides in a near-silent drum solo, apparently weighing something carefully in his mind. Paul followed him, patiently waiting for an answer.

"She's fine," Alyec said at last. "She's *safe,*" he corrected himself, choosing more precise words, "from the man who was trying to kill her—and everything."

"That's all I needed to know," Paul murmured. "Thank you."

"Hmmph," Alyec said, a little annoyed at his admission.

"Could you—could you let her know that we miss her? And worry?"

"I think she knows already, but I'll get word to her. You're her best friends." They stopped in front of the comic shop and he frowned pensively, not really looking in the window but perhaps at something more distant. "I think," he said slowly, "Wonder Woman's breasts are pointing different directions in this poster—aren't they?"

Paul desperately hoped that if Chloe was involved in some international conspiracy/drug/gang/corporate espionage/murder thing, Alyec wasn't a key agent. He was nice enough, but he sure was lacking in the brains department.

Ten

"Hello?"

"Amy? It's Chloe."

She sucked in her breath, waiting for Amy to react. There was half a second when there was no noise from the other end.

"Ohmygod, Chloe! Where the *hell* are you?"

Chloe relaxed. This was the Amy she knew. Pissed as hell, but the same good ol' Amy.

Chloe was in her new room, sitting on the floor up against the wall by her bed. She figured if anyone caught her, she could just tell the truth: that she was telling her friends she was okay. No one had told her specifically not to call *them*. And she could always play the stupid-sullen-teenager routine if she had to.

Of course, why was she even worrying about that? These people, *her people*, had accepted her and protected her and taken her in with love and enthusiasm—no questions asked. She was even wearing really comfy

79

yoga pants and a top that had been quietly provided for her—correct fit and all. Why was she suddenly worried about being *caught* or doing the wrong thing?

Chloe twisted a piece of her dark hair around her finger. It was time to get it cut soon—another thing she'd neglected with all the excitement of the past few weeks.

Unless it turns out I'm a shorthair. She almost laughed at her own joke.

"I'm with some people—they're protecting me from the people who want to kill me." Chloe flinched, realizing how stupid that sounded.

"What the hell are you talking about? I thought it was just that one guy! Was that mugger part of this, too? Are these gangs? Are you in a *gang*, Chloe?" Before Chloe could answer, Amy started shouting, sounding muffled, as if she was holding the phone to her chest. "It's Chloe! She says she's all right. I think she's been kidnapped. No, I'll tell her." The barely audible masculine voice that was answering back was definitely Paul. "Just get on the other phone!" Amy snapped.

He's over at her place. Late, Chloe realized.

There was a click, then Paul was on.

"Hey, Chloe." Calm as ever. She wondered, not for the first time, if anything ever ruffled his feathers. "You okay?"

"Yeah, I'm fine, Paul."

"Cool. We were worried about you, you know."

"I know." She smiled but felt a little strange. She was

glad that Paul seemed to accept her safety as a matter of fact and that he believed she could handle anything she was in the middle of right now. It was great that *some*one had that kind of confidence in her. But didn't he care enough to crack his cool exterior just a little? Shouldn't he be just a tiny bit more worried?

"Anyway, I have *not* been kidnapped. And it's not gangs—" Chloe thought about the Tenth Blade and the Mai. Strip down their history, legends, occult origins, and secret powers and, well, actually . . . "Okay, it's sort of like gangs. But it's also sort of international and stuff. . . ."

"I *knew* it!" Amy cried triumphantly. "Alyec's a spy for the KGB, isn't he?"

"Learn a little history, will you?" Chloe snapped, finding herself falling back into her old pattern with Amy instead of this being the I'm-okay-I-love-you call it was supposed to be. She took a deep breath. "This has nothing to do with the Cold War—" But then again, it sort of did. "Okay, there's these two groups—the Mai, who are basically related to me, and the Order of the Tenth Blade, who are sort of all about killing the Mai because . . ." *Think this one out, Chloe.* "Because the Mai were sort of a hunter-warrior caste who were . . . undeservedly reputed to be bloodthirsty and . . . animalistic. It's all really old and stuff. The important thing is that Alyec saved my life when that psycho from the Order tried to kill me." Well, that wasn't *exactly* true—he had held Brian at bay while she fought the Rogue, and the truth was that maybe Brian really *had* been trying to help her. . . . But if Alyec hadn't shown her the things he could do as a cat, she would have been slit from nose to navel immediately by the Rogue's daggers.

"He didn't," Amy said, obviously not wanting to believe her.

"He *did*," Chloe repeated firmly. "And more than that. These people are going to help me find out who my biological family is. They might have all been killed—" She thought about Kim with a faint gleam of hope, then wondered how she and Amy would get along. Chloe decided not to mention her potential sister just yet. "But they might still be alive. These people are dedicated to finding all of the people from Abkhazia, a country in the old Soviet Union, who were scattered and bringing them over here safely."

"Sounds like they brought trouble with them," Amy observed. Chloe opened her mouth to argue, but in a way, her friend was right.

"Come home," Paul suggested. It was *almost* a plea. "As soon as you can. I don't trust these 'people.' "

"Yeah, they probably tapped your line."

"Amy, this is a cell phone. . . ."

"Whatever! Don't be a douche. When are you coming *back*?"

It was a strange question. Chloe had only been at Firebird with the Mai for a week or so and it already felt like a completely new life. Sure, she missed her mom and Paul and Amy, but the thought of suddenly waking up tomorrow and going to school again was just weird.

She paused too long, trying to figure out how to answer it.

"So you mean you haven't even *considered* coming back," Amy said evenly.

"Not until it's safe," Chloe said, faltering.

"And when's that?" Paul asked. His voice was beyond cool. "When this Order thing has been completely wiped out? When they're all dead? How many of them are there? I mean, it sounds like a real gang war, from what you're saying."

She hadn't thought about it.

She *really* hadn't thought about any of it.

She thought about it now, though, sinking into her pillows. They kept saying—*Sergei* kept saying—she could go back "as soon as the danger had passed" and Chloe just accepted it, repeating it, making it the truth by repetition. What did she expect? That the Tenth Blade would just give up after a while? That they would grow bored with hunting the supposed killer of one of their Order? That there was some sort of statute of limitations on accidental death in the middle of a five-thousand-year blood feud?

Did she really believe that one day Sergei was going to come to her with an all-clear signal, hug her, let her go back home, and insist that she drop by once in a while? Now that she thought about it, no one ever acted like she was going to be leaving at any point. Alyec never said anything one way or the other. She had a *job*, for Christ's sake.

"I don't like the way this sounds, Chloe," Amy said grimly. "I want to see you. Myself. If these people are so great, they shouldn't mind letting you see your friends."

"Amy, now is not a good time. . . ."

"I mean it! Promise you'll meet us. Or I'll call in the cavalry. I call the police. *I'll tell your mother.*"

"All right, all right, I promise!" Chloe agreed.

"When?"

"I don't know! I'll call you again when I can, okay?" She looked at the battery meter. About a quarter left. She didn't have a charger with her and for some reason, once again, she didn't feel comfortable asking for one. Come to think about it, no one in the Pride knew about her phone except for Alyec—and now Igor and Valerie— so unless they told anyone, that was it. Why did that make her feel better somehow?"

"All right. Call me by Saturday or it's the cavalry. I mean it."

"All right! I'll see you later."

"'Bye!" Paul shouted.

Chloe flipped her phone closed and looked at it for a long time, sitting on the floor.

"Well, that's . . . weird . . . ," Paul said, distractedly arranging Amy's stuffed animals into extremely lewd positions.

"Stockholm syndrome," Amy answered promptly, pleased with herself. "She has begun sympathizing with her own kidnappers. She's beginning to really believe they are keeping her safe instead of just keeping her."

Paul looked up at her and narrowed his eyes. "Amy? What are you planning?" he asked evenly.

"Nothing," Amy said, crossing her arms. "Yet."

But they both knew it wasn't true.

Eleven

"Well, well, my own son wants to have dinner with me," Whit said, folding the painfully white linen napkin into his lap. "What an extraordinary honor."

Brian grimaced. Once again his father had managed to turn the tables so everything was to *his* advantage: Mr. Rezza had chosen the Ritz-Carlton's restaurant for dinner, much to Brian's dismay. It embodied everything that Brian did *not* want to get involved in during their discussion. Fussy place settings, crazy rich people, annoyingly perfect and subdued lighting, silent waiters, and worst of all, a dress code. *Technically* Brian wore the required "business attire," but he saw that the maitre d' was pissed at his Generation-Y interpretation: brown velvet pants, a leather suit-style jacket, and a Diesel shirt that he wore with a thrift store tie.

"Shall we start with a bottle of something? Maybe some Krug Grande Cuvée to celebrate the occasion?"

Brian had an almost overwhelming urge to point out

that he wasn't old enough to drink, but now was not the point in the conversation to start acting up.

"Whatever. You know I like reds."

"Oh, that's right." Whit looked at his son with something approaching fondness. "I remember: cabernets. A strange thing for a California boy, but I don't disapprove. I seem to remember they have some very nice native ones here. . . ." He took out a pair of reading glasses and buried his nose in the wine list.

Brian sighed. At least his father seemed a *little* nervous despite his posturing. It had been several months since they had really spent any time together outside the dusty walls of the Order's chapter house. The older man looked more or less the same, maybe a little tanner, maybe his jowls were just a little bit tighter. He had said something about taking up squash or tennis. He was a large man, imposing, with an utterly patrician face and a nose that was large enough to make him look regal but sharp enough so that he looked like he was something other than a hundred percent Italian. Only his easy olive tan betrayed a Mediterranean origin.

His outfit was impeccable, a several-thousand-dollar Armani suit that fit so well with the shirt, the cuff links, the tie, and the shoes that except for the slight paunch, Brian's dad could have been a model for some older men's magazine. Whitney Rezza was a living embodiment of taste and wealth well spent.

"Dad," Brian said, clearing his throat, "I think we should consider me leaving the Order."

His father looked over the wine list at him.

"Don't be absurd."

Brian had thought long and hard, and the best thing he could do for Chloe now was to cut all ties with the organization that was bent on killing her. Whatever happened between the two of them, he would be free of the Tenth Blade, and Chloe would feel confident that she could trust him.

But that was only partially it: this was also an opportunity for Brian to figure out what to do with his life. Which he knew, regardless of anything else, did not involve the Order of the Tenth Blade. At best it was a silly society of archaic rituals and secrecy; at worst it was a group of people devoted to killing other people. Either way, it was not going to be his life's work.

"I'm serious, Dad. I want a career, an education—I want a *life*." He ran his hand through his own thick dark hair, angry at his own nervousness.

"All of those things are possible while you remain in the Order," his father said, slowly setting the wine list down, "if that's what you really wish."

"I want to *concentrate* on 'those things.' I don't want to have to run out of a final because of some emergency meeting the way Dickless—uh, Dick did a couple of weeks ago."

"Richard is an extremely devoted young man,"

Whit said patronizingly. "He is an exemplar for the Order."

Then why don't you just adopt him and be done with it? His father's feelings toward Dick used to drive Brian up the wall; now he *wished* his dad was grooming the college student for eventual leadership. God knew he himself didn't want it.

Brian took a deep breath.

"Dad," he said patiently, "most people *choose* to join the Order. Even Edna—"

"That's *Mrs. Hilshire* to you, Brian."

"Even fucking *Mrs. Hilshire*—" He stopped when his father gave him a warning look. "Even *she* gave her kids the choice. Evelyn chose to join, and William and Maurice didn't."

"Well, I don't have the luxury of *three children* and the chances that *one* may follow in his father's footsteps. I only have *you*."

"It's not my fault you only have one kid," Brian snapped, his temper slowly getting the better of him.

"Oh, is this where you're about to blame me for the death of my own wife again?" his dad said, annoyingly lightly. "How if it hadn't been for me, she would still be alive? How I might have had three kids, and you would get out of your current predicament? You're right. Terribly selfish of me to let my *own wife die*. I didn't realize how it would inconvenience you."

Brian's foot began to shake under the table. He

forced himself to stop it, not wanting his dad to see how close he was to losing control.

"I'm not talking about that." *Though I should throw it in your goddamn face, you self-satisfied* . . . "I'm talking about my right to choose my own life."

"Sometimes we don't have those choices, son. Look at Prince Charles," Mr. Rezza said gravely. "Listen, I inherited this burden from your grandfather, just as he did from *his* father. Sometimes we just have to accept what we're given and bear it manfully."

Manfully? Brian almost cracked up. But it *was* interesting that his dad had phrased it that way. Was it possible that Whit Rezza had rebelled at some point? That his own father had shot him down? Brian's grandfather seemed like a gentle enough old man, but Brian knew there was a sharp and possibly evil mind behind his friendly exterior.

"I understand that, Dad," Brian said softly. "But these are different times. I have . . . individual rights, like the right to pursue my own path."

He knew as soon as he said "individual rights" that he had made a mistake. The almost-caring look his father had given him disappeared, replaced with a stony glare.

"Nonsense," he said with disgust. "Your generation has no sense of responsibility to a group, a calling higher than your own. You treat random friends like family and family like strangers. You want to dither your life away, pursuing one pleasure after another. That is not a *path*; that is a waste of life."

And that was that. Brian had tried to sail the choppy waters of his father's limited common sense—and failed. Mr. Rezza picked up the wine list again.

"Everybody in the Order has had their doubts at one time or another, Brian, even Edna. Even myself. It's an inevitable phase in the path to becoming a fully integrated member. You'll get over it." He paused, his eyes scanning the wine list. "What about a merlot?"

Twelve

Still sitting on the floor long after she'd hung up on her friends, Chloe picked up her jeans that were wadded in a pile. There was a wear spot threatening to tear into a rip. It was already tissue thin. She ran her finger over it and the harder nubbles of the denim around it. These were vintage Lees she had saved for herself at Pateena's.

"I expect to see you back on Wednesday—if not, don't bother ever coming back." Her boss's words echoed in her memory.

Chloe sighed. Her job at the vintage store was just another thing her new screwy life had, well, screwed up. She had an overpowering urge to talk to Marisol, the owner and her friendly boss—if Marisol was still her boss, that is. The older woman always seemed to understand Chloe better than her mom ever did and sense her moods with an uncanny knack. Even if she couldn't tell her all her secrets, Chloe had always unburdened some of her feelings. Now, of course, that would be impossible.

Hi, Marisol. Sorry I flaked and didn't come to work after you gave me that last chance. I know I'm effectively fired, but there were good reasons. I can't really tell you why, but can I just vent for a while?

The sadness of a relationship ended fought for space in her head alongside her anger at the thought of Lania—her work nemesis—running the cash register all the time now.

Chloe prepared herself for a nice introspective and lonely sulk on her bed, but she was too nervous. Too energetic. Like that night that seemed so long ago, when she'd run out of the house and gone out to the club.

But then again, cats and lions weren't known for their mixed feelings or inaction. They just *did* things. She was upset, and she had to do something about it. Right then.

They wouldn't miss her for a *few* hours, right?

Waltzing through the front door was out of the question. But a glance out the window revealed a ledge and all sorts of nooks and crannies in the brick and stonework that were perfect for someone with claws. Using both her arms and a little force, Chloe raised the window until there was an opening high enough for her to get through. Cool, moist air entered the room. There were the scents of pine and mud and something so clear and snapping that she could only think it was like the moon.

How could Sergei spend all of his time in the old house? True, it was gorgeous and huge, but as a Mai, how could he resist the call of the outdoors?

She looked around one last time. Was she betraying the people who had let her in? Maybe she could talk to them and they could arrange some sort of escort for her so she could visit her mom safely, or Paul and Amy, or even Brian. . . . But she had to see her mom. *Now*. It hit her with an overwhelming urgency.

Without another thought, she pitched herself through the window and crouched on the sill, just barely touching her fingers to the wood for balance. Her feet itched inside her sneakers. Though the Sauconys' grip was great for running, Chloe suspected she would have an easier time climbing down with bare feet, her toes curling around the stones. She untied her sneakers and tossed them back into her room, under the bed. Her socks followed.

She wiggled her feet, now free, and was somehow unsurprised when claws extended out the tips of her toes, just like Kim's. She extended her hand claws and leapt, unsure what she was going to do as she fell but confident she would figure out something and positive that she would land safely.

And she did.

Chloe didn't even think about what she was doing as she shot down, as fast as she'd fallen off Coit Tower. She landed lightly on a lower gable. There was a quiet, high-pitched squeak of her foot claws against the stones. With only a moment's pause to grin at what she had done, Chloe scurried from curtained window ledge to curtained window ledge, one story at a time, letting her feet dangle and then drop down.

When she hit the lawn at last on the back side of the house, the grass was cool and wet and almost silver. With her night vision, she could see her own footsteps on the turf: slightly darker impressions where the balls of her feet dissolved the individual spheres of dew, causing them to blend together and sink into the ground. It was such a beautiful and fascinating discovery that Chloe had to force herself to look away and continue on with her journey.

No wonder you always catch cats staring at nothing for hours. I bet they see a billion little things.

She ran with her body against the walls of the house, trying to get to the woods as fast as possible. She tried a couple of test leaps as if she had four legs, stretching her arms in front of her and pushing off with her legs. Sort of like the way Gollum did it in *The Lord of the Rings* movies. It worked, but not too gracefully, and didn't seem to help her pick up speed. The Mai were one hundred percent upright walkers.

Which made her wonder about what Kim had said. Were they really a race created by ancient gods? Chloe still didn't quite believe it, but what if it were true?

Then again, what if the Order of the Tenth Blade was right? What if they weren't created by benevolent ancient gods, but by demons? What if they *were* demons of some sort?

But she had tried to help the Rogue after he tried to kill her. Chloe wasn't evil. Was she?

She let go of her thoughts and refocused on her present. She ran, and yards of ground disappeared under her strides. She felt herself slip into the shadow of the pines. No one could see her if she didn't want to be seen; she *knew* this. And if she had to, Chloe could easily live out of doors full time, in the trees, like a child's fantasy of freedom.

Her cat imaginings fell short as she ran along the edge of the driveway and came to the road. It didn't take more than a second to figure out how to scale the fence when the gatehouse guard had his back turned, but once she was on public streets again, she suddenly realized that even with her Mai speed, there was no way she could run all the way to her house, chat with her mom, tell her everything was okay, and get back in less than a few hours.

Feeling a little defeated, she took a bus over the Golden Gate, from the edge of Sausalito. She sat in the back, trying to keep herself from bouncing, only remembering to retract her claws at the last instant. No one took much notice of her bare feet; this was San Francisco, and with the wild look in her eyes and her barely contained energy, she easily passed for either a strung-out junkie or a riot grrl on the way to her next rally.

Chloe got off the bus when it crested around Golden Gate Park, preparing to run the rest of the way. She decided to take a somewhat circuitous route in case anyone was following but didn't go too out of her way because time was short.

In the end, it didn't matter.

She passed a surprisingly healthy looking street person—she would remember that later and curse herself for it. As Chloe gave him a wide berth, he turned to look at her. Their eyes locked, and she suddenly realized there was something far too sane and directed about him.

Just as she was about to move even farther away, he raised an ornate wooden club and smashed it down at her.

Chloe threw up her hands and claws to deflect it, but the club was moving so swiftly and the man who wielded it was so strong—and prepared—that she only managed to keep the tip from hitting her head.

It made a cracking noise as it hit her collarbone instead, but most of the impact was taken on the side of her neck.

Chloe fell down, pain and fear shooting through her at the same time. She tried to get to her feet, but the pain and feeling of *wrongness* in her neck kept her from moving properly.

Another person appeared over her.

He wasn't another "homeless guy": just a normal-enough man walking a tiny dog, distinguished only by his bright orange sweater.

"Help me!" Chloe cried, lifting her hand to him.

He reached for her, but then she saw that he held

something black and ropy that Chloe couldn't identify. As his sweater tugged up his arm, she saw the tattoo, the same one the Rogue had had : *Sodalitas Gladii Decimi*.

Chloe screamed. Her claws came out and she slashed at her captors wildly despite the overwhelming pain.

But both of her assailants were well trained, if slower than the Rogue. The one dressed as a bum put his knee on her chest, forcing all of her air out. He grabbed one of her arms while the guy in the sweater grabbed her other.

"Going to visit your *mommy?*" he asked nastily.

She kicked. this was something they were not prepared for. While Chloe couldn't reach the one crushing her ribs, the claws of her left foot shot out and neatly got sweater man dead in the stomach. He screamed as she felt his flesh gather up and tear beneath her claws. But she still couldn't breathe, and silver stars began twinkling at the edges of her vision.

Then somebody hissed—and it wasn't her.

Suddenly the weight was lifted off her chest. She sucked in as deeply as she could and was rewarded by a scorching pain that was so great it masked the pain from the wound on her neck. She could see again, although what was going on was mostly a blur: there seemed to be two other people, faster than the Tenth Bladers, attacking and pummeling them with an eerie silence.

Chloe sat up as best she could. They were Mai, of course, although she didn't recognize them. Their movements and their scent were unmistakable. They were *big*, too—which made their silence even scarier. Homeless guy landed with a thump next to her, his eyes blank with unconsciousness. Chloe lost her temper for just a moment, finding the urge to slash his face almost overwhelming. Instead she dug her foot claws into his crotch. When he woke up, he'd have something to remember her by.

Then she collapsed back on the pavement.

"I *knew* she was going to be trouble," one of her saviors sighed, walking toward Chloe. This was a woman; she was dusting off her pants. With a casual kick she stilled the "homeless" guy, who had begun to moan and twitch.

"Can't blame her. She's a kid," the other one, a man, said. It might have been Chloe's delirium, but the two looked very similar. "Besides, I haven't had this kind of fun since August."

The woman was scanning the night. Suddenly she dropped down, crouching with one hand for balance, the other pointing. "More coming."

"Bring 'em on!" the other said. Then he added, "I know, I know."

"You grab her legs—careful of the neck. It might be broken."

"Where's our glorious pride leader?" the man asked with heavy sarcasm. "*This* wouldn't even have cost him a life. Assuming he *has* more than one."

"Shhh! Keep it to yourself, Dima. The girl might still be conscious."

She is, Chloe thought, before fainting entirely.

Thirteen

They weren't traveling in the land of the warm sun anymore, of endless sky and sand. They were someplace colder and wetter, with incredible mountains and a very different sea, very close by. She walked through the streets of an ancient city. Stones of buildings centuries dead stuck out of the ground.

Few people paid attention to her. The markets were crowded with people from all over. One of her shadow companions sniffed the air disapprovingly, wrinkling her nose at the stink of the hordes. She smiled down at the four silent lions. "Let us find our orphans and move on from this place."

They turned a corner and a shadow fell over the five Mai; one whined as the stink of rotten eggs became overpowering in the wet heat of the afternoon sun. . . .

"Chloe?"

She opened her eyes. Sergei's face was uncomfortably

close to her own, and he looked concerned. His breath stank of garlic, which was not the smell in her dream at all but still made her sick.

Chloe was lying in her own bed at the mansion. There was cloth mounded tightly against her neck, wet with melting ice. She tried to turn her head—it was possible, but the pain was searing.

"Maybe you'll listen to me about visiting your mother next time?" he said gently, patting her on the hand. It was a little rough, the action of someone who wasn't used to showing affection. Chloe blushed and looked down, too embarrassed by her disobedience and its result to look him in the eye.

"I know you miss her," he continued, "but the Order wants you dead, Chloe girl. You took out one of their best—and craziest—soldiers. They knew you would try to go home at some point. Every exile does." His white-blue eyes looked beyond her for a moment, into the distance at something else.

He really does sort of look like a lion, Chloe reflected. *If his reddish-silver hair and beard were drawn back from his head—and just a little longer—it could be a mane.*

"All you're doing right now is endangering her. Give it time, let us help work things out, and we'll reunite the two of you eventually. Okay?" He patted her on the head.

"Okay," Chloe agreed, smiling despite herself. "I'm sorry."

"Don't be too sorry—Ellen and Dmitri had fun for the first time in a while. And neither of the criminals they took out will be causing any more trouble for a *long* time." He grinned, showing a mouth of teeth as short and square as himself. "Enjoy yourself, Chloe girl! You're a teenager who doesn't have to go to school for a while. At your age I would have loved such a thing."

She nodded, and he adjusted the sheets around her, tucking her in.

"Will I ever be able to go home?" she finally asked, sounding more pathetic than she meant to.

"Of *course* you will, Chloe," he said fondly. "We do not mean to keep you here forever—although, of course, I'd like to." He smiled and chucked her under the chin. His teeth were very carefully divided by the black lines separating them, Chloe noticed. It was a strange, perfect little grin.

"How is it ever going to be safe?"

"Ah. Well. Five ways," he said. He held out five fingers and counted them down. "One: Someone finds the Rogue. This is still possible—it takes a lot to kill one of those bastards and no one actually saw him hit the water. Two, and this is far less likely, we have a *true* détente and convince them of your innocence. They do not really consider us human—I mean, intelligent rational beings—and almost never agree to meet, but it has happened once in a great while. Three: We make things very difficult for them; tie their hands with other methods. Like a police investigation. Or, even worse, an IRS investigation. Or an accidental 'explosion' at one of their weapons factories."

"Weapons factories?"

"Yes. They skirt the law themselves a lot, these so-called protectors of the innocent. Four"—he coughed to show a sense of embarrassment where there wasn't really any—"we could threaten the family of one of the Order. I know," he said, putting up a hand and closing his eyes as Chloe started to say something, "this is an idea alien and horrible to your young, naive, human ears. But Chloe, they don't play by fair rules, either. Why else would they hunt an innocent teenage girl like yourself? Why would they send the Rogue after you to begin with?"

Actually, now that Chloe thought about it, why *had* they? She hadn't become a threat to anyone until *after* she'd had to defend herself from that psycho, when the Mai had sent Alyec to teach her how to defend herself. It was a chicken-and-egg situation.

"They sent someone after you because you were an easy target," Sergei said sadly. "You weren't part of a pride, you weren't part of a group who could protect you. It would have been an easy way for them to pick off a member of the Mai with no risk and few repercussions. They have done this before with other orphans like yourself—you should ask your friend Kim about it sometime. We found her hiding in an alley, living in a box in the garbage."

Chloe could see it, although she didn't want to. A little girl with black hair and bright green eyes, terrified, keeping to the shadows and hiding in piles of trash so the men hunting her wouldn't find her.

"Trust me, Chloe," Sergei said, a hard look coming into his face. "As someone who lived in a very dangerous part of Eastern Europe at a very dangerous time, survival is difficult and often unpleasant." His finger went up to a corner of his eye and scratched there, apparently of its own accord. Chloe had never noticed it before: part of his right eyebrow was especially kinked, and there was a very slight line where what looked like two different pieces of flesh had been sewn together to cover a wound.

"There was a fifth way," Chloe whispered. "You said there were five ways it could be safe for me."

"Ah. Yes." Sergei snapped himself out of his thoughts and looked at her both sternly and pragmatically. "That would be if one of us was killed by them in the next few weeks. Then we would be even." Chloe sucked in her breath.

With that, he left.

Chloe tried flexing her shoulder again. More pain, but still not so bad. Her neck wasn't broken, and neither was her collarbone. She noticed a glass of water on the night table next to the bed and a dish with two ibuprofen, which she immediately scarfed down. She grabbed the remote and fluffed up her pillows, preparing for a good afternoon of daytime TV. Then her hand hit something—her cell phone, which she had stashed there the night before, when she went out. She pushed the power button and saw that there was a message waiting from an unrecognized number. She called her voice mail as she began switching channels, looking for *Jerry Springer*.

"Chloe, it's Brian again. Listen to me—whatever you do, wherever you are, stay there for the next couple of days. The Order has blanketed the streets around your house with members looking to bring you in—one way or another. *Don't* try to visit your mom or your friends. I'll try to talk to you later."

Chloe checked the time the message had come in—8:12. Almost an hour before she had gone to try and visit her mom. If she had left her phone on, she would have gotten the call and avoided the fight.

Chloe thought about this, and Brian, for a while, looking up at the ceiling and finding little lion images playing in the knots and whorls of the wood there. They seemed to twist and jump, dancing like lions in the wild. . . .

Not ibuprofen, she realized, sinking into unconsciousness.

"I *told* her she was all fat and nasty—nobody would want her. I didn't know there were guys like Joey who liked *bleep* like that."

Currently there were four of the largest women

Chloe had ever seen on the TV. One woman didn't seem to have a neck at all, even when Chloe paused the TiVo to get a better look. Another had been to the hospital and had a fifty-pound tumor removed, without ever having realized it was there. Next to them were the men who loved them and across from them the siblings who reviled them. Now *this* was television.

When she had woken up, Chloe had been determined *not* to think about anything important or deep again for a while, but just to take advantage of being a sick little girl, recuperating in front of the TV.

Kim appeared at her door, silent as ever.

Chloe beckoned her in but held up a finger: the fat woman who had just been insulted was getting out of her chair and waddling over to try and hit her attacker.

"What's this?" Kim asked, coming over to her bedside and looking at the TV curiously.

"*Jerry Springer,*" Chloe replied, shaking her head as it took four stagehands to pull the woman away from her sister.

"It seems sensationalist and distasteful," Kim said, wrinkling her nose. Chloe started to laugh, but then paused.

An ad came on and Chloe shut it off. "What's up?"

Even with Kim's alien features, it was easy to tell she was disappointed by something. She sat on the edge of Chloe's bed, gripping the covers with her foot claws for balance, and waved a manila folder of papers.

"I don't think we are related." She said it calmly, but Chloe could see her eyes flicker. "As far as the genealogical people have made out, you more closely resemble the Mai who fled to Turkey from Abkhazia in the nineteenth century. My family stayed in what is now Georgia."

Chloe didn't understand half of what she was saying. "You mean I'm Turkish, not Russian?"

Kim fixed her with a cool look. "You are Mai. Not 'Turkish' or anything else. There are no *human* nationals of any sort in your background."

Chloe had forgotten about that. She was a completely different race. Wonderful, colorful images of herself in scarves, black kohl eyeliner, and bangles, with belly-dancing music in the background—like at the restaurant her mom used to take her to—sadly faded.

"Is this my file?" she asked.

Kim shook her head. "No, it is a sort of general file with information on places we are all most recently from. I thought you would be interested. St. Petersburg, where Alyec is from." She passed Chloe pictures of an exotic city, with spires too long and thin to be mistaken for those of American churches. Onion domes dotted the skyline. Everything seemed to be covered in gold like a fairy-tale kingdom.

"What's this?" Chloe pointed to one of the other photographs, of a building with a wall of large white stone blocks. A woman was walking along it, a woman with long black hair. "It looks familiar. I saw it in a dream." She suddenly felt the crowded market street again, the shady, quiet alley with the horrible smell.

Kim looked at her strangely but turned the photograph over. "It is one of the old sulfur bath complexes in Sokhumi. This part of Abkhazia was a famous retreat with spas—the natural hot springs and mineral water there were supposed to have curative powers."

Sulfur . . . This is a little too weird.

"Does sulfur smell like rotten eggs?" she asked, afraid of the answer.

"Almost identically." Kim put the photograph down and looked Chloe in the eye. Her black velvety ears lay almost flat against her head, turned backward. Chloe couldn't tell if she was upset or listening for footsteps in the hall. "You dreamt that, too?"

"Yeah. It was humid, and there were people, and . . . it was kind of confusing. Modern and ancient at the same time. And it *stank*. But I remember that wall."

"Sokhumi is the city where our pride eventually settled after we left the Middle East for good. Only one of the Mai from that diaspora came *back* to Abkhazia—our previous pride leader. Her dream was to gather all of the scattered Mai in Eastern Europe and unite them somewhere, like the United States." She carefully put the photograph away and closed the folder. "But she was killed in a skirmish between the Abkhazians and the Georgians."

"There were other exiles, from all over, who rested and waited for her," Chloe murmured.

"What did you say?" Kim demanded, fixing her like a mouse with her eyes.

"In my dream I *was* the pride leader."

"That's . . . interesting," Kim said slowly.

"Do you think I could be related to her?"

Do you think she could be my mother?

Kim opened the notebook again and looked at the picture of the bathhouse in Sokhumi again. "It's possible. . . . But she had only one daughter that we know of, and she is dead. . . ." She sounded reticent, and somehow Chloe didn't think it had anything to do with the disappointment about the two of them not being related. There was something else. . . .

Maybe she was jealous of Chloe possibly being the daughter of the old pride leader. Maybe it meant something, like inheritance in an aristocracy. Maybe she would take over when Sergei's term was over. She wondered if that entailed anything besides running a real estate empire and tracking down lost and orphaned Mai.

What was it the two guards had said when they were rescuing her? *Where's our glorious Pride Leader? This wouldn't even have cost him a life. Assuming he has more than one.*

"Kim—before I went unconscious, one of the people who rescued me said something about the pride leader not risking losing 'one of his lives.' What did she mean by that?"

"Traditionally, in the past, the leader of the Pride is

also a true military leader, first into a battle or on the hunt, last to retreat—" One of her ears flicked. A moment later Chloe heard the noise, too: footsteps echoing loudly down the corridor. It sounded like Olga; she was probably coming to check up on Chloe.

Kim leaned close in, too close for a normal human. Kind of like Amy's cat, when he would push his nose and foul-smelling kitty mouth into Chloe's, smelling delicately around her face before withdrawing. "Listen to me, Chloe. *Do not tell anyone about your dream or what we spoke of,*" she hissed. "There are leaders, and there are *leaders,* Chloe King."

Fourteen

Paul might be complacent and all best buddies with Alyec, but Amy wasn't going to stand for it. If it were up to her stupid boyfriend, they would just sit back and do nothing until the world fell down. Which was exactly why she was skipping out of school early.

She'd given a half-assed excuse to her teacher about feeling sick and hadn't even bothered going to the nurse. Her brother's car was parked in the area of the lot reserved for seniors, and it had cost her an arm and a leg to borrow it: a guaranteed okay on any future favor of his choice. *It's not like he even needs it at Berkeley.* It was an ancient, all-black Chevy Malibu station wagon that he called the Batmobile. The Malibu was a pretty small car for its V6, though, so when she floored it, the car tore out of the school parking lot like a bat out of hell.

Amy zoomed through the streets and parked several blocks away from Chloe's house. She locked the car and went up to the front door, trying not to look around suspiciously, trying to make it look like she had every right to be there, pulling out Chloe's spare key and entering the house in the middle of the day when they both should have been in school.

Mrs. King usually came home around seven, and Amy had every intention of being out of there in an hour. Maybe she'd even go back to school. . . .

On second thought, who did she think she was kidding?

She had been planning this for several days and wore an appropriate outfit for breaking and entering (even if it was with a key): tight black jeans and a black tee, along with a black Emily sweatshirt whose hoodie had cat ears and sleeves that ended in gloves with claws. Perfect for a cat burglar. She had admired herself in the mirror for a while that morning. It was such a completely different look for her—all sleek and black. None of the crazy, bouncy, fringy, fluffy stuff she designed and wore. Her breasts stuck out a little bit; they almost looked as big as Chloe's in this outfit. What she really needed was a pair of long black leather boots à la Emma Peel and maybe to dye her hair black, but Paul didn't like it when she changed her hair color—he'd always liked the original shade.

She carefully closed the door behind her and listened for a minute. If anyone was staking out the place, there was no sign: everything looked fairly normal in the King household. No furniture was overturned, nor was there any other sign of violence. Just to be safe, however, Amy pushed herself up against the wall and slid toward the stairs, ducking when she got in front of windows, doing a crouching run up the staircase.

Which resulted in a very non-cat-burglar trip on the top step and a flying fall that nearly smashed her chin against the bathroom door. Most of Amy's life was spent trying to *get* noticed and stand out; this sneaking thing was entirely new to her. She pulled herself up into what she hoped looked like a shadow and tiptoed into Chloe's room.

Once again everything seemed normal, maybe a little dustier than usual but not noticeably changed. Chloe's computer was properly shut down. Amy turned it on, using the special black gloves so she wouldn't leave any fingerprints. She admired them while it booted up, then went online and logged onto Chloe's e-mail—her friend had had the same password for years: adopTED5.

Aha.

Chloe religiously purged her trash to keep her mailbox from going over its size limit, downloading and saving all of the particularly juicy letters in case her mother ever found her way on. She did *not*, however, empty her sent mail folder as often as she should—and was far too painstaking about adding names to her address book. After just a couple minutes of poking around, Amy found brian9@bitsy.net and, searching Chloe's "locked" Word documents, confirmed that it was *the* Brian that Chloe had been interested in.

115

Amy then signed off and switched Hotmail over to one of her own alias accounts—one that she used when she didn't want to be found, for contests and spam and mailing lists and stuff—and sent Brian an e-mail. Early on, Amy had decided to handle everything Chloe from foreign computers, not her own, in case someone was capturing her IP address.

Brian: This is from one of Chloe's friends. Where is she? Can you help us? Alyec seems to know something but won't tell. E-mail me ASAP.

Then she made sure it sent properly, deleted it out of the sent mail, and purged the trash. She checked it again to make sure it was really gone, cleared Explorer's cache for temporary files, and started to even defrag the hard drive—to *really* make sure all the information was gone—but looked at her watch and realized it would take twenty minutes. So Amy shut down, mission accomplished, and prepared to sneak back out.

Just like out of the movies, she was halfway down the stairs when the phone rang. Amy froze, flattening herself against the wall so hard that static electricity lifted her frizzy red ends straight up against the wallpaper and her shoulder almost dislodged a picture. She waited, frozen, knowing intellectually that it was okay to move but unable to make herself. She scanned the room until voice mail picked up, counting the seconds.

She noticed something that she wouldn't have if she had just snuck immediately back out. *Nothing in the house looks moved.* Like for a while. There was a stillness to it, and though there were no layers of dust, there was a palpably stale feeling about the place. It even smelled a little old, like the garbage had been sitting there for just a day or two too long; there was no tang of cleaners or soap or perfume or anything that connoted movement or life in a house of two women.

Shaken by this realization, Amy left the house less carefully than she'd entered—after all, she was only human, which was exactly what the people watching her exit the house wanted to be sure of.

Fifteen

A new loving family, a secret race of people like her, no more school ever again, and all Chloe could think about was how bored she was. Her "internship" at Firebird mainly involved stuffing envelopes, making copies, collating large stacks of contracts, and taking orders from the obnoxious Mai receptionist.

While she was waiting for a stack of . . . something, she wasn't sure what, from Igor, Chloe thought about her and Amy's dream of setting up a shop somewhere. Amy would design the clothes and Chloe would run the business. Assuming the two didn't kill each other, it would be a match made in heaven.

Igor must have seen the look on her face.

"You should become a full-time paralegal," he said, smiling.

"Wow. This for a living," Chloe said deadpan, tapping the stack he was adding to. "That would be just great. For my *entire* life."

"Remember, it is hard for people like us to integrate completely," Igor said seriously. "That's why it was so good for Sergei to set this up here." He was wearing khakis, a button-down with a fashionable tie, and suede shoes. The way he leaned back in his chair and clasped his hands behind his back made him look like any young professional: a little bit arrogant, but bright eyed and smart.

Pity about the name. Maybe assimilation would have been easier if the Mai hadn't named their kids after horror film characters. With just a slight tilt of her nose to the air Chloe could tell he was Mai. It wasn't a smell, exactly, but a feeling.

"Is this why he's pride leader?" she asked, waving her hand around the office.

"He is pride leader because when the previous one was killed, he bravely took up her mission of trying to reunite the Eastern European Pride." Chloe wanted to jump in and prove her knowledge to the older boy by saying yeah, yeah, the Abkhazian Diaspora, etc., but decided maybe it would be a good idea to pretend to know *less* than she did for once.

"He organized everyone after the Georgian violence, and when he immigrated, he began the process of bringing us all over. Sometimes legally, sometimes not so legally." His dark eyes were shining with admiration. "And he built all this—an *empire* of city real estate— from nothing, an immigrant! And a Mai. So in a way, yes, it's about all this but more, too."

120

"Seems pretty nice," Chloe said, meaning it. "So why does Alyec bitch about him not helping *his* family out?"

Igor chuckled. "Alyec is a whiner. Perhaps there is some prejudice—but the ones in St. Petersburg, Moscow, and even Kiev were better off than the Abkhazians. Sergei wanted to help out the most desperate first."

"Oh." She looked around for something to do now that their conversation was over. Her foot tapped spastically.

"I know what you need!" Igor said, suddenly popping up out of his chair and pointing at her. "You are all itchy and nervous and bored. You need a " He suddenly looked around and trailed off. "A hike," he finished lamely.

"Oh. Boy. That will fix *everything*," Chloe answered with as much sarcasm as she could muster. Currently she was wearing a pair of expensive jeans—probably picked out by Olga or Valerie—that were a size too small around her crotch, so she had to leave them unbuttoned and wear a big, stupid, trendy wide leather belt around her waist. The sweater was light pink cashmere. She still had her Sauconys, but everything else wasn't hers and didn't feel like hers. Like her room, like her new family, like this crappy new part-time job—which didn't involve clothes *or* a cash register.

"Good," Igor said, taking her at face value.

Chloe wasn't sure if it was being Mai or Eastern European that prevented everyone there from getting sarcasm.

★   ★   ★

She had dinner that night with Sergei. It had become their little ritual on days that he worked late: she would come to his office and he would clear his desk. They would order Chinese, pizza, whatever they were in the mood for, and play a game of chess. Chloe never thought she would be good at it, but she was slowly learning. She treasured these evenings no matter how much she hated losing.

She wondered if her real father—her *adoptive* father—played chess. She couldn't even imagine thinking about her real, *real* father. . . .

"Igor told me I should go on a 'hike'; what does that mean?" she asked after moving a pawn.

"A hike? I haven't the slightest idea." Sergei blinked at her with surprisingly innocent eyes. In his emotions and movements, he seemed *very* childlike sometimes— maybe that came from being in his forties without a wife and children. "*Oh!* He means a hunt. Ah, that Igor, he is a smart one. I think they are organizing one for this Saturday. Do you know anything about raising wild-cats—bobcats, cheetahs? For pets?"

Chloe had no idea what this had to do with anything, so she shook her head. Sergei got up and came around to her side of the desk and sat on its edge, looking at her seriously, like he was giving her a very important father-daughter lecture. Chloe prepared to be bored, but it was sort of a nice new feeling.

"People up in Oregon and other places raise wild cats to sell. Some make great pets, like bobcats and lynxes, if they have been bred and raised properly by a loving family. But no matter how gentle, well behaved, and obedient a cat is, no matter how much regular cat food he can stomach—once a month the good breeders throw a live chicken into the pens and let what happens happen."

Chloe felt nausea rise as she imagined feathers and blood and screams.

"They have to do this, Chloe," he said gently, "because you cannot completely breed out a cat's basic nature. They need to hunt, they need to play with their prey, and they need to kill. We are no different. We have always been hunters. Nomads. We never grew our food; we went after it in the wild.

"If you feel anxious and trapped—if you have the urge to *run* at night and chase and follow—you need to give in to it once in a while. We cannot run free like we used to before the world grew civilized and the land was fenced off, but we must still obey the ancient instinct."

Chloe suddenly understood part of the Tenth Blade's credo. A Mai gone mad with hunt lust in a city or town probably *was* a dangerous thing. She decided to keep that thought to herself, however; somehow she suspected Sergei wouldn't share that conclusion.

"So we do this every month? Go hunting?"

Sergei laughed. "Not *every* month, Chloe. It has nothing to do with the moon, or your feminine things, or clockwork. Sometimes it's just . . . time to go."

★ ★ ★

Time to go.

Chloe thought about this while she waited by the Ford Explorer. It was dusk and they were on top of a hill somewhere near Muir Woods. It was a sharp hill, new and ridged, not like the older storybook rolling hills on the way there. A bright star shone in the south, although how Chloe knew the direction was south, she couldn't have said. Below, the land ran steeply down to a bowl of forest and scrub with smaller hills within it, like the bottom of a scenic snow globe. But instead of plastic flakes, darkness gathered at the bottom.

About a half-dozen Mai were there, speaking in low voices. They were all women. Olga and Valerie were there along with three she didn't recognize, one of whom she knew was Simone, the dancer who also lived at the mansion. Chloe never saw her in its halls.

Most of the women seemed to be in their thirties. They were all beautiful. They all had high cheekbones and thick, shiny hair; even with the different eye and hair color and body shape, it was easy to see a racial similarity once Chloe began to look for it.

One of the things they all had in common was how inhumanly they walked: standing mainly on their toes and moving with a careless precision that could have only been carefully choreographed by a human ballerina.

A dark-eyed woman Chloe didn't know began the evening with a chant, a strange hymn in a foreign tongue that went from low whispers to beseeching cries.

Her voice was good but alone and sometimes lost in the breeze—which made it even creepier. Chloe caught the name Sekhmet once or twice, but that was about it.

Afterward they were silent.

"I have a scent!" one of them hissed. She had yellow eyes, orange hair, and a round face that resembled Sergei's but a cool, high forehead and neck that could have easily gotten her on the cover of a fashion magazine. She wore a tank top and had tattoos of leopard spots ringing her upper arms.

They all cocked their heads, sniffing the air. Chloe did, too, and when the faintest breeze changed directions, she had it: a musky scent that made her think of herbivores, even though she wasn't sure she had ever precisely smelled anything like it before.

A deer. They were going to run down a deer.

The redhead who'd first caught the scent pointed and the rest began running, following the direction of her finger. Chloe paused, thinking about the mountain lion attack on a jogger that she and Brian had argued about just a few weeks before. He had insisted the lion should be put down for attacking a human; she had suggested the unfairness of humans moving in and destroying the lion's habitat.

Now she wondered if the attack had been by a lion at all.

The air tickled her nose again: the deer was farther away. *Getting away.*

She ran. Her companions were rarely visible: once they descended off the top of the hill and into the edge of the woods, the Mai darted in and out of shadows, keeping a more or less straight line along the scent of the deer but out of sight of anyone or anything that might be watching.

Clouds raced across the sky as fast the hunters beneath them. They slipped from the moon, and the blanketing shadows parted for just a few seconds: the bushes and trees went from gray and purple to white and silver-green, then faded back as the foggy curtain closed again. Chloe felt her legs pumping smoothly below her. Her arms moved at her sides as though they were pushing the air behind her to speed her up. Her lungs felt like bursting, but the air was light, inspiring her to run harder. Chloe leapt over a bush and laughed. *This is what it's supposed to be like.* Running with a purpose, running with her pride.

She paused for a moment to smell the air again and continued: they were catching up. Even though they were two-legged, they were running down a *deer*. A cat's growl sounded behind her. Chloe didn't answer. She went where her senses told her: to a clearing up ahead, a long field in the open. Chloe could feel the closeness of the brambles begin to give way to something that was open to the stars.

She came out suddenly, before she could stop herself. Momentum caused her to almost tumble over the rock she paused at—a beginner's mistake. She saw the deer. It, too, had paused and was flicking its long ears left and right. It seemed to look right at Chloe with big dark eyes, but she knew that if it actually *saw* her, it would have begun running again; the Mai were downwind from it. The deer was beautiful, and Chloe could barely wait for it to begin running again so they could resume the chase.

The deer must have heard something; it suddenly turned and leapt, a beautiful four-legged spring from a standstill that Chloe had only seen on nature programs. The smell of the terrified animal hit her nose with a slap, and before she knew it, Chloe was running again.

She saw her companions emerge from the bush and silently nodded at them in greeting as the pack drew up into a close formation, the redheaded girl taking up the rear. The deer flashed into darkness and the six women plunged after it into the woods, where Chloe could hear nothing but her own breathing and heartbeat, not a footstep of those around her.

They shot out into the bright moonlight again—the doe was only twenty feet in front of them. One woman pulled ahead with a series of springs and leaps that were so far from human that anyone watching would have been hard-pressed to recognize her as a form of sentient life.

Chloe suddenly realized what was going to happen.

They were on a *hunt*. There was the deer, there was the hunter.

She stopped running and turned her head, covering her eyes.

The girl before her let forth a cry—it was *Valerie*, Chloe realized, a little stunned. She put her hands over her ears and waited, unwilling to experience anything of what she knew had to come next. Her chase lust vanished.

"Hey, not a bad first hunt, eh?"

Chloe opened her eyes. One of the other women approached her, speaking gently. She was in her late thirties, as fit and taut as a circus performer. Her long hair, tied back for the chase, now swung freely to her waist. Her accent was pure Californian; she must have been here even before Sergei. "No rabbits, not a lot of blood—are you okay?"

"I'm just, uh . . ." Chloe wasn't sure what she wanted. "It's all a little, uh . . ."

"You feel better than you did before—the night you tried to sneak out?" She said this with a grin.

Chloe opened her mouth to snap back at her, but now that she thought about it, Chloe realized she really *was* a lot more relaxed. She still wanted to see her mom, but the insane urgency was gone.

"Yeah," she answered slowly.

"Here." Valerie came by with a bottle and handed it to Chloe. "To the hunt and your health!"

Chloe eyed the rim carefully, looking for bits of blood. Then she tipped it and took a huge swallow of the ice-cold, perfectly smooth vodka. The women's laughter rose on the smoke of the campfire up to the stars above them.

★   ★   ★

They returned to the mansion at seven or eight the next morning. It was like nothing Chloe had ever experienced before. The six of them spent the night laughing, talking, singing, passing around the vodka, and cooking deer steaks. It was like one of those New Age women-power touchy-feely weekend getaways she had seen in movies or in ads for antihistamines, completely unselfconscious and natural. She had tried a little bit of the deer—it was very different from the venison she'd once had at a restaurant her mom had taken her to, tougher and more gamey tasting. Nothing she would go out of her way to eat again, and now that the chase lust was gone, she couldn't help thinking about the doe's eyes and face right before they'd killed it. It made her feel a little sick or, at the very least, not so hungry.

Some stayed up all night and some—like Chloe—had dozed off. She should have been cold, but the campfire was warm, and she found she could just pull her arms into her shirt and retain her heat that way. She thought about the desert in her dream and how cold it must have been at night.

When she awoke, she had the feeling that there had been lions in her dream again, but she couldn't remember what had happened. There was just a vague lingering presence of a familiar warmth and coarse, honey-colored fur.

When they came in the next morning, Chloe felt achy but good, like she had hiked a mountain or had a really good workout. A couple of the women brought the rest of the deer into the back and finished butchering it or doing whatever it was they had to do, but Chloe went straight to the kitchen for coffee and a muffin—she was starving.

Kim was there, blowing delicately on a mug of green tea. Chloe wondered if there was *anything* the girl did that wasn't healthy, pure, or proper.

"How was the hunt?" the other girl asked politely.

"Great . . . I think," Chloe added. "I'm surprised you didn't come along—it seems right up your alley."

"I'm not sure what I think about it."

Chloe looked at her in surprise. The girl with the cat ears, slit eyes, and claws didn't know what to think about a *hunt?*

"I have given the matter a considerable amount of thought and prayer and meditation," the girl explained, seeing Chloe's expression. "We are hunters, yes—but the time of *needing* to hunt for food is over. Should we still do this and kill? Or would the gods consider it a waste?" Kim shook her head. "I don't have an answer yet." And she padded silently out of the room.

Chloe frowned, more confused than ever.

Sixteen

Amy and Paul were at his house, actually studying together for once. Amy sat on his tiny twin bed, Paul on the floor next to her, her legs often wrapped around his shoulders. Sometimes he would lean over to kiss her calf . . . and another half hour would disappear before they got back to work. But on the whole they were fairly productive. The room was quiet, much quieter than in Amy's household, and Mrs. Chun came up occasionally with a plate of cookies and to "make sure they weren't doing anything"—although she was obviously kind of hoping they were. Compared to his cousins, Paul was an extremely well-groomed, hygienic, cool dresser . . . and Mrs. Chun was a fanatic devotee of *Queer Eye for the Straight Guy*. She'd come to her own conclusions about her son, concerned that the divorce was somehow screwing him up.

Everything was still very neat in Paul's house but light: things were missing that Amy couldn't quite put her finger on, some essential furniture or spirit seemed to be gone. The Chuns were polite and amicable when it came to dividing up their possessions, but the whole place was a testament to their separation. Depressing.

Paul's iMac made some backward-sounding music noise, recognizable only to Amy as a tune by Siouxsie and the Banshees. "Mail for me!" she cried, leaping up and almost taking Paul's head off as her feet hit the ground.

"Who is this? You've been checking your mail all evening. You got another boyfriend or something?" Paul asked, straightening his shirt and looking back at his book. Amy clambered onto the stool in front of the two-by-three-foot wood board that passed for his desk, kept immaculately clear of the hundreds of books, records, and CDs that crowded the rest of the room. She hit enter twice: her account had no password on his computer; she had no secrets.

Her eyes widened when she saw the address of the sender.

"It's from *Brian*." She took her purple pen and wound it through her hair, sticking it down the middle of the knot to keep it all up off the back of her neck.

"Brian who?" Paul asked, not really interested. Then he looked up, realizing. "Brian *who*?"

"Chloe's Brian."

He couldn't see her face, but Amy flinched, waiting for the inevitable.

"Why is he e-mailing *you?*" He put his book down and got up to stand behind her and read over her shoulder.

Amy, you and Paul need to STAY OUT OF THIS. You're safer not knowing any more than you already do. Your lives could be endangered.

I don't know where Chloe is, but I've had word from her that she's safe.

Brian

P.S. Don't talk to Alyec about this anymore either.

"Where did you get his e-mail address?" Paul asked, wanting to solve that mystery before he tackled any of the other number of issues this missive brought up.

Amy sighed. "I cut out of school early on Wednesday and went over to Chloe's house. I broke into her computer. I also e-mailed him from there."

"You did *what? Why?*"

"Because Alyec won't talk, Chloe's still missing, and we still don't know *anything!*" she said, beginning to feel less defensive and more pissed off. Her blue eyes flashed and she stood, putting her hands on her hips. It would have been a far more effective gesture if the pen hadn't chosen that moment to pop out of her hair and fall to the ground.

"Besides that message from Chloe herself, two people have already told us she's safe—two people close to her. What more do you want?" Paul said, his voice also rising.

"What do you mean, 'two'?" Amy asked, frowning.

Already caught, Paul didn't have time to retreat into his blank look.

"What do you mean, *two?*" Amy repeated, pushing her face closer into his. "Brian and *who?*"

"I talked to Alyec," he finally admitted, "after you totally accused him of everything. I talked to him calmly and rationally, and he told me that she was fine, and he would tell her that we were worried about her."

"Oh, so *that's* how it is?" Amy shrieked. "You approach Alyec all man-to-man like after your hysterical girlfriend screws everything up and he just tells you everything?"

"It worked, didn't it?"

"Assuming he's even telling the truth. Why didn't you tell me?"

"Why didn't you tell me about your little breaking-and-entering routine?"

They both fell silent, staring each other angrily in the eyes. Then they both looked away. The answer to both the questions was the same: they were afraid the other was going to disapprove and freak out over it.

Which was exactly what had happened.

Then Paul laughed. "I can't believe you actually broke into the Kings' house."

"I know where the key is," Amy admitted sheepishly, also smiling.

They were quiet again, too full of their own thoughts

to say anything, for the second time that evening—and for the millionth time that week.

"When I was there? At Chloe's?" Amy began, quietly and more calmly. "It was weird—like it hadn't been lived in for a while. Nothing was messy, but it just had this *stale* feeling. A little dusty or something." She screwed up her eyes, trying to think about the last time she had been there, before they'd walked across the bridge, the last time they'd seen Chloe. "I don't think the glasses near the sink were washed," she hazarded, "but I'm not sure."

"Too bad they have voice mail," Paul said with a wry smile. "You could have seen if the answering machine light was blinking out of control with all the calls we left her. I don't suppose you have their password for *that*, do you?"

"No," she pouted. "If I did, there are a lot of messages I left over the years that I would have erased an hour later, when I calmed down."

Paul smiled and ran his hand up through her hair at the base of her neck. Amy closed her eyes and pushed her head back into his hand.

"Maybe it's time we called Mrs. King at work," he suggested quietly, picking up the phone.

Amy looked at him in surprise, then at her watch. "It's ten after five—she'll definitely be there."

He dialed and Amy pressed her head to the other side of the phone.

"Greenston and Associates," the receptionist said in a deep, interested, expensive-receptionist voice.

"Hello, can I speak with Anna King, please?" Paul spoke in an even voice. His tone might have been youthful, but the sound was polite and professional, something Amy never could have accomplished.

"No, I'm sorry, she's away on vacation this week. Can I help you or direct you to another lawyer?"

Amy and Paul looked at each other.

"Uh . . ." Paul cleared his throat. "Where did she go?"

"I'm afraid I can't divulge that kind of personal information," the receptionist said regretfully. "I hope it's someplace warm."

"When will she be back?"

"She has a *lot* of vacation time saved up, so I'm not exactly sure precisely which day—would you like her voice mail? She often checks it when she's away."

"Uh, thanks anyway. It's nothing urgent. I'll call back in a couple of weeks."

"Thanks for calling."

He slowly hung up the phone. Both of them stared at it.

"*Now* can we do something?" Amy finally demanded.

Seventeen

This was a different sort of dream, restless and real. It was daylight and silent; Chloe's feet made no sounds in the harsh grass beneath her feet. The broad blades cut into her soles, but it didn't matter. The only thing that mattered was the hunt. She saw her quarry on a rolling hill below her, a familiar doe who paused to watch a plane overhead. There was something wrong with that, but through her thickened mind Chloe couldn't figure it out.

With two powerful leaps she flew over yards of scrub, landing in the middle of the perfect road that separated her from the kill. The pavement was velvet black with solid yellow lines and seemed to focus all of the sun's heat on her. She prepared to leap again.

The deer turned toward her, as if it had known she was there all along.

"Chloe," it said, in an achingly familiar voice.

Chloe froze and screamed, but no sound came out.

★　　★　　★

She sat up suddenly in her bed—no, the couch. It was the middle of the night—no, she checked her clock and it was only seven thirty. *Another nap,* she realized. Chloe had drifted off to sleep again while she tried to plow through *The History of the Mai.* It was Bible thick and combined all of the confusing names of a Russian novel and the deadly dullness of a badly translated history text. She fell asleep fairly easily these days; if she was full, warm, and not immediately occupied, it seemed like sleep was the inevitable next step.

Chloe rubbed her temples with her knuckles. The doe in her dream had spoken with her mother's voice.

It was the scariest nightmare Chloe had ever had.

Just a few weeks ago she'd been fighting with her mom, making up, going to work, and hanging out with her friends. And now she was . . . *not.* She fingered the soft, richly colored velvet spread she had slept on. She squinched one eye shut, noticing how she could suddenly see all of the individual furry threads in different shades of ruby, like through a magnifying glass. Then they turned darker and matted down, sucked up into the weave of the fabric, as her tear was slowly absorbed by it.

She sat up again.

"I have to get out of here," she said aloud. "I want . . ." She couldn't quite figure out what she wanted. She ran a hand through her hair. A haircut? Some new vintage clothes? She leapt up and ran out of the room, suddenly terrified by the silence.

Out in the hall she slowed herself down, embarrassed by her behavior. Then she pulled her cell phone out of her back pocket and turned it on. Technically she didn't need to use it for *this* phone call—no one cared; in fact, they probably encouraged her speaking to Alyec. Only an eighth of a battery left and she had to talk to him *now*.

"'Alloo?" he asked, accented, as if he expected someone Russian to call.

"I need to go out," she said without preamble.

"Chloe!" She could hear the happy boyish grin on his face. Simple, just glad that she had called. "Didn't you just go out on a hunt?"

"I don't want . . . ," she growled, shaking her hands in frustration. If she couldn't make *Alyec* understand, she was doomed. "I just want to go out and do something *normal*. Fun. You know? *Fun?* Like a date?"

"I don't think Sergei will let you out alone with me. I'm a pretty strong boy, you know, but not a trained bodyguard."

"Okay, okay." Chloe thought furiously. "We'll make it a *group* date. He can't object to that, can he? A bunch of us—whatever goons he wants to send along with us—we'll *all* go out. To a *movie* together. How about that?"

She fell back against the wall and slid down until she was sitting on the floor. "I just want to go out," she said miserably. "I want to eat popcorn." *Not wild deer.* "I want to drink a blue slushy, watch stupid previews, and use a crappy public bathroom with ugly tiles and mirrors that show all my zits."

There was a long pause at the other end. She waited for Alyec to ask about that last thing—she wasn't sure why she had said it but remembered when she and Amy used to go in before and after a movie and make faces and put on lip gloss. Amy would complain about the size of her nose, wrinkling it, and Chloe would bitch about getting breasts too early.

He didn't let her down.

"I'll see what I can do. But your skin is perfect, Chloe. You have no zits."

Sergei said he couldn't refuse a thing to his adoptive daughter, which was how Chloe, Igor, Alyec, Valerie, a couple of the kizekh—the same ones from the other night—and Chloe wound up sitting around the lounge with the entertainment sections of different newspapers.

And Chloe was reminded how, no matter what your race was, whether you were human or Mai, trying to get more than three people in a group to decide on a movie was a royal pain in the ass.

"I would like to see *The Russian Ark*," Valerie said. "It's still playing at a couple of art houses."

The two guards nodded in approval.

"Kiss ass," Chloe muttered.

"Well, okay," Valerie admitted gamely. "I would rather see the new Hugh Grant movie."

"Is Julia Roberts in it?"

"No, but Reese Witherspoon plays his niece. . . ."

"No, thank you," Alyec said, sticking his tongue out in disgust.

"How about *Hills of the Dead*?" Igor asked.

"Yeah!" Alyec agreed, leaping, Mai-like, onto the back of Igor's chair and looking over his shoulder.

"Absolutely not," Valerie said, sticking out her jaw—a lot like Amy. "Horror movies freak me out."

"That's the point, dumbass," Alyec said. "I hear Raymond Salucci did the score," he added to Igor, who nodded excitedly.

"It's gonna suck," Chloe said hesitantly. Honestly, she didn't mind—but Valerie did look really upset.

"How about *The Return of the King*?" the other girl suggested, offering a compromise.

"I've seen it four times already," one of the guards replied, shaking his head. Chloe shot the scarred older man a look. He just shrugged. Although she was almost positive that he was one of the ones from the night she'd been ambushed by the Tenth Blade, the other kizekh, the woman, had called him "Dima," but tonight he had introduced himself as "Dmitri," and she was pretty sure that was the name Sergei had used, too. She didn't know what the woman's name was. *Living here is worse than being in a Russian novel.*

Chloe scanned the newspaper, hope dwindling. She didn't really give a rat's ass what they saw—as long as she was out, at a movie, with crowds of normal people around her. *Well,* she thought as she eyed the two guards, already standing protectively behind her, *somewhat farther around me.* The guards had their arms crossed like storm troopers.

"Hey!" She suddenly had an idea and flipped through the newspaper, looking for the right ad. "The Red Vic always shows *Star Wars* at midnight on the weekends."

"I thought it was *Rocky Horror,*" Igor said.

"Theater one. Theater two always shows *Star Wars.*" She finally found the ad, the sort of cheap, tiny five-line text-only ad that gave away the theater's independent nature. "Yep. Midnight tonight."

"Fine with me," Alyec said, still balancing on the back of Igor's chair.

"Okay," Valerie agreed.

"Absolutely!" Igor grinned, big, thick white teeth showing for the first time since . . . well, since Chloe had met the serious young man. Even the two *kizekh* nodded. Who, after all, could say no to *Star Wars?*

"Let's get ready and be back here in an hour," Igor said, looking at his watch. "An *hour,*" he added, giving Alyec a look.

"That still gives me time to kick your ass in Soul Calibur," Alyec said with a sweet smile. Valerie rolled her eyes and gave Chloe a look. Chloe smiled back, sympathizing. But she felt pretty sure that *she* could kick Igor's ass at it, too.

"You're on," Igor agreed, suddenly leaping up so that his chair tipped backward because of Alyec's weight, sending the other boy flying. But he did a neat little flip in the air and landed on his toes and one hand—somehow reminding Chloe of Nightcrawler in *X-Men United*. *Who needs movies when you are a mutant?*

She went back to her room to brush her hair and grab her jacket. The only makeup Chloe had with her was cherry-tinted lip gloss. She put it on as thickly as she could and mourned the fading of her healthy skin to a pasty paleness from being inside for so long. She grubbed her cheeks and pinched them hard, remembering something out of *Gone with the Wind* or some other old movie. It gave her a little color; she hoped it would last.

Kim was padding silently upstairs as Chloe headed back to the lounge, reading a book she held before her with the deference of an ancient monk reading his hours. The brown tunic-length sweater with bell sleeves that she wore did nothing to detract from the image.

"Hey," Chloe called, catching up to her. "Want to go to a movie? A bunch of us are going."

Kim looked at her as if it was the strangest thing she had ever been asked.

"Thank you," she said slowly, "but I have some reading to do   "

She said it unconvincingly.

"Come *on*," Chloe said, exasperated. "It's a Friday night. You have exactly jack shit reading to do. I don't

143

care *how* homeschooled you are; classes are over for the day, chiquita."

Kim looked her over again, curious about Chloe's strange energy and goodwill. *I certainly haven't displayed a lot of it since I came here,* Chloe realized.

"I haven't been to a movie in a long time," Kim hazarded, closing her book.

For some reason, Chloe couldn't imagine Kim *ever* going to a movie. "Great. Get your coat. Come on."

"Do the others know you're asking me?"

She said it in the same infuriatingly calm, even tone she always used—which kind of reminded Chloe of Paul—but there was a catch in her voice this time, the subtlest swallow. Her eyes were large, her pupils so wide that you almost couldn't tell they were slits.

The armor of the pious scholar had just cracked a little, and Chloe felt a rush of pity for the poor girl, aloof and alone. But if she did or said anything that was the slightest bit patronizing, it was all over.

"No, but I totally think there's enough space in the cars." She had no idea if this was true, but it was the *correct* answer. Kim looked relieved at Chloe's brashness, the assumption that everyone would just do what she said—and let Kim come—without question.

"I'll get my coat, then, and meet you in the lounge."

"Uh—what about your . . . ?" Chloe indicated her ears, not sure what to say. "I mean, is it going to be all right?"

Kim gave what was almost a smile through her teeth, pointy and sharp. "Yes. They always just think I'm some freaky goth kid."

Chloe smiled back. "Right on," she said, holding her fingers in a peace symbol.

Now that she thought of it, why *did* she just assume that the others would go along with whatever she said? Chloe wondered at her behavior as she went back to watch Alyec and Igor. Why would anyone disagree? Did people think Kim was that much of a freak and a pariah?

Alyec was jumping up and down, moving his body with the game pad, using his claws occasionally for a tight move. He threw his entire body into the game. Igor sat stock still, a serious look on his face, fingers barely moving across his own game pad. And he was royally kicking the other boy's ass. The two guards, looking almost like CIA agents, stood in the background, quietly waiting.

"Hey," Chloe said. She threw herself onto the couch with one leg over the side. "I just ran into Kim. She's gonna come with us."

"You're kidding," Igor said, but all his concentration was on the game.

Valerie came in, looking like a movie star. The cat was very strong in her, and even without Kim's eyes or ears, there was a barely contained power and sensuality beneath her features. Her eyes were heavy-lidded, like Sergei's, but with long lashes and a smoldering look. She slunk like a cat, too, smoothly and languidly. Her hair was lighter than Alyec's, an almost Marilyn Monroe blond. But natural.

Chloe tried to work up a little envy, but it was hard: she admired the other girl too much.

Of course, the fact that she had seen her take down a deer bare-handed might have something to do with the whole lack-of-envy thing.

"Ah, crap," Alyec said, throwing down the game pad as Igor executed his fatality. "You lucked out."

"No," Igor said easily, sliding back to put his hand on Valerie's knee, "you just suck."

"I'm ready," a voice said behind them.

Everyone in the room turned. Kim stood, all bundled up in a fake black fur coat that went down to her knees. A black baseball cap was pulled down over her ears. Giant black Doc Martens, several sizes too big to fit her foot claws, clunkily covered her feet. She looked a little defensive.

"That's a . . . very interesting outfit," Valerie said, as tactfully as she could manage.

Kim gave her a cold, dismissive look.

"I don't think we can fit everyone in the Explorer," one of the guards said.

"That's okay," Alyec said smugly, drawing on his leather jacket. "I have a car with me."

"Oh no," Chloe realized. "It's *not* . . ."

But he just grinned.

*   *   *

146

It *was*, in fact, the exact same hatchback he had stolen before from the senior running back at school. Igor and Valerie went with the two guards, muttering something about Alyec's proficiency at driving.

"This is your car?" Kim asked, getting into the backseat without being asked.

"Don't ask," Chloe recommended. "And buckle up."

"It's . . . very nice," she said doubtfully, unconsciously imitating Valerie's earlier comment.

Chloe checked the rearview mirror a couple of times to see how the girl was handling it, but Kim looked steady no matter how fiercely Alyec took the turns; she had one hand braced on each side of the car and swung between them, bouncing.

"This is great." Chloe sighed. "This is just what I need."

"I'm glad." Alyec leaned over and kissed her on the cheek. Except for their occasional sort-of dates, they had actually been far less physical in the last week than . . . well, ever. Sergei never said anything aloud about his feelings toward Alyec, but it was obvious there was a tension between them and some invisible line her boyfriend could not cross. But it didn't feel like a normal "don't date my daughter" scenario; Chloe got the feeling that if it were anyone besides Alyec, it might have been okay. She made a mental note to ask someone about that sometime—maybe Olga.

"Hey, Kim," Alyec yelled to the backseat, trying to be sociable. "You ever see *Star Wars*?"

"Of course I've seen *Star Wars*," she snapped; the *you idiot* was understood.

There was a long pause.

"Who's your favorite character?"

Chloe caught the girl's eyes widening.

"The . . . ah . . . furry one. Not only do his physical characteristics set him apart, but the . . . obvious subservient dynamic between him and the . . . uh, *protagonists* indicate his role as either a hero-ally or comic-mentor archetype."

"So what you're saying," Alyec said philosophically, squealing around a corner, "is that you've never seen *Star Wars*."

Kim glared at him. Chloe was glad their cat abilities didn't include anything like shooting lasers from their eyes. If they had, Alyec would have been fried.

"No. I have *not* seen *Star Wars*," Kim admitted, then looked out the window so she wouldn't have to look at them.

Chloe laughed.

In the theater she wound up sitting between Kim and Alyec, since he and Igor and Valerie all insisted that since *Chloe* had brought the other girl, she had to sit next to her. Actually, it wasn't so bad. Kim was inordinately pleased with the popcorn, another humanlike thing Chloe had a hard time comprehending. But the girl with the hidden cat ears relished every bite, using her claw to spear one kernel

148

at a time and carefully deposit it on her tongue, never taking her wide, unblinking eyes off the screen.

Igor and Alyec shouted lines with the characters and other lines *at* the beloved heroes with the rest of the crowd. Valerie and their two guards watched it in silence. Chloe had to answer a lot of whispered questions from Kim but didn't mind; she knew the script by heart and found it kind of fun to initiate a newbie.

"What is that they are on?"

"A consular ship."

"*Space*ship?"

"Uh, yeah. Starship, really."

And:

"Why is everyone cheering? What is the significance of that being a space station and not a moon?"

And:

"Stupid Alyec. I was closer than I thought. This story taps perfectly into Western archetypes—from the hero to the quest to the tragic hero. It is right out of Joseph Campbell. In fact, there are even parallels between it and the Egyptian story *The Tale of the Shipwrecked Sailor*. . . ."

"So, in the other movies, do they reveal Darth Vader as being Luke's father?" Kim asked casually, picking up a flyer and looking at the upcoming releases.

Alyec's jaw dropped. "How did you know that?"

"It is pretty obvious, if you know anything about mythology and religious tales," she answered smugly. Chloe grinned, then noticed Igor trying to win a stuffed animal from one of the claw vending machines for Valerie. "Hey, win me a toy, huh?" she demanded, handing Alyec a dollar. Then she pulled Kim after her into the women's room.

"I don't have to go," Kim protested.

This is so not like Amy. Chloe sighed. She would just have to make the best of it. She pouted into the mirror and applied more lip gloss. Kim watched her without saying anything, taking off her baseball cap briefly so she could scratch her ears.

"Hey," Chloe suddenly said, remembering. "What was that you were going to tell me the other day? About the pride leader?"

Kim looked startled. She licked her lips and tried to speak didactically, but something was worrying her. "Um, just that the leader of the Pride has to be the first to charge in and the last out of battle. The leader has to stay to defend the weakest, run into a burning house to save the slow. The leader gives his or her life for the Pride. Up to nine times, if necessary."

Chloe laughed. "Like a cat, you mean? Like . . ." Then she suddenly noticed how grim the other girl looked. "You're *serious*," she realized.

"A true leader proves him or herself," Kim said quietly. "It comes out in battle. In war. In times of danger and catastrophe. Usually leadership runs in families. Sometimes a Pride gets lucky and several warrior family members rule together. But sometimes it does not;

sometimes a person rises up in a time of need when there is no one else. And is killed and rises again."

"Pride leaders have nine lives?" Chloe repeated slowly, to make sure she understood.

"Not all . . . *pride* leaders. But true ones do. It is what protects our race."

Coit Tower. Her fall. The dreams. The lions. "This *wouldn't have cost him a life. Assuming he even* has *more than one."*

Chloe opened her mouth. "Are there . . . uh . . . others? Who can do that?"

"Well, there were," Kim said almost mournfully. "As I told you, the only daughter of our pride leader—the one before Sergei—was murdered before she had a chance to prove herself, and no one else of this generation has shown any signs. *Or* risked their lives to find out."

Kim was gazing steadily into her eyes. Chloe blushed and turned away. She couldn't deal with this now. *Pride leader?* But sooner or later, she was going to need to think about what Kim had said.

When they got home, Chloe went immediately to Sergei's office. It was very late, but he didn't have normal sleeping patterns, and she wanted to tell him what a great time they'd had . . . and maybe talk about finally getting to call or see her mom. She would have said something to announce her presence, but about four Twizzlers were crammed into her mouth. Alyec claimed he had won them from the prize machine at the movies. Twizzlers were definitely *not* one of the prizes—only cheap stuffed animals and plastic jewelry and stuff like that—but Valerie said that apparently Alyec had spent an additional five dollars to the one that Chloe had given him trying to get her something and had finally given up and gone to the concession stand. Chloe had laughed—that was definitely something lighthearted and stupid that someone like Brian would *never* do.

The older man was standing behind his desk, talking urgently to one of the upper-ranked Mai in his company and two of the kizekh.

"So we agree. She presents too many liabilities, I'm afraid. Something will have to be done to remove her—"

He suddenly noticed Chloe, his blue eyes fixing on hers without recognition—for just a second. Then he warmed up. "That's all for now, gentlemen. Thank you." All three nodded at him in a way that was practically a bow and almost backed out of the room facing him, as she had seen Olga and Kim do.

"What was all that about?" she asked, sliding into one of the enormous chairs that no one had been sitting in.

"Someone who is not working out at the company," Sergei said quickly, shuffling papers together on his desk and sitting down. "We will have to let her go."

"Why did the goons have to know about it?"

"They are not *goons*, Ms. King. They are highly trained warriors." He and his adoptive daughter locked eyes for a moment. Then he sighed. "It is not about an employee, you are right. It is about a member of the Order of the Tenth Blade we have to try to eliminate. I am not just the leader of a company that employees my people, Chloe: I am also pride leader of the Mai. There are ugly and distasteful things that go along with such responsibilities."

Chloe nodded, but her mind raced. She had never seen a female member of the Order. That didn't mean there weren't any, and she had certainly never seen any of its leaders, so maybe she was someone in charge. But usually someone used the term *liability*—at least in the movies—to mean someone on the *home* team. Like someone who has some good points who still has to be gotten rid of.

Not me, right? The thought flashed through her brain, and Chloe tried to hide her concern.

Chloe *did* present extra danger to the Mai, especially with her stupid stunt the other night. But no, there were too few of them left for the pride leader to just randomly go around and have them murdered.

"These are tough decisions," he went on, "things that hopefuls like Alyec don't understand. Things that make a man old before his time."

"Alyec?"

Sergei chuckled. "He is one of the ones 'in line' should something happen to me. Or at least that's what he thinks."

"Why not Igor? Hey . . . do you have any Sprites?"

"Perhaps Igor. There are many good qualities about him," Sergei said, reaching into the mini-fridge by his desk and taking out a couple of cans. He passed one to Chloe. "He is responsible and serious—but he is going to be married soon. Some would say he lacks a certain, ah, *aggression*. He is more of a president than a CEO, if you know what I mean."

Chloe nodded, concentrating on opening her can and making a Twizzler into a straw. There was too much new information to think about.

"I'm feeling a little hungry—what do you think about half sausage, half pepper?" he asked, punching the number for the pizza place on his phone. Chloe nodded again. Then he noticed her inserting the Twizzler into her Sprite. "Chloe, whatever are you doing?"

Sergei had enjoyed learning how to bite off both ends of a Twizzler to make it into a straw and laughed heartily about how you were really supposed to do it with cheap champagne. They'd had a nice game of chess—he'd beat her roundly, of course, but gently—and he'd told her all about growing up in the Communist Soviet Union, both the food lines and the amazing education and intellectualism that Chloe had only read about.

When they left, he gave her a bear hug good night, but as soon as she began heading back to her room, the uneasiness she'd had about the meeting she'd interrupted came back. For the first time ever, the term *cult* came to her mind. Not that there weren't actual reasons in this case: they were a different race, completely set apart. But that didn't change the suffocating totality of the Pride; even when Chloe was allowed to do normal things, like going to the movies, it was with other Mai. She was completely cut off from the rest of the world.

When she got back to her room, Chloe opened her phone and dialed. She had left too many people on the outside worried for too long. It was time to see her family and friends. But she would do it differently this time, intelligently. Far from her home and the watching eyes of the Tenth Bladers.

"Brian? I have to see you. . . ."

Eighteen

The next day Chloe was still thinking about her mom, Paul and Amy, even Brian.

"Hey." Chloe knocked on the temple door as she walked in. As expected, Kim was there in the corner, meditating or reading a book or something.

Kim must have detected something in her tone, because when she looked up, one of her eyebrows was already cocked and suspicious.

"Can you do me a favor? I want to go out and meet a friend—a human one. Would you mind providing an alibi? I'll tell Sergei you're, like, instructing me in the way of the Mai or our history or the twin goddesses or something." She tried to make it sound as casual as possible. "That way the goo—uh, kizekh won't follow me."

You want me to cover for you, Kim said in her even, toneless voice.

"Yeah," Chloe said uncertainly; she had no idea what the other girl was feeling.

"All right," Kim agreed just as tonelessly; she flicked her ears once and went back to her book.

"Hey, thanks! I owe you one."

The other girl just grunted, not looking up again.

Chloe turned to go, not sure what to do, feeling like the interview was over.

"I really enjoyed last night," Kim suddenly said unexpectedly, eyes still glued to whatever she was reading. "Thank you for inviting me."

This was about as much joy as she was ever going to get out of Kim, Chloe realized. She smiled. "No problem. We should totally do it again."

She turned to go but couldn't. Chloe realized she had already asked way too much of Kim, but the question had been gnawing at her since the possibility had been raised.

"So, uh . . . did you find out any more? About my parents? If my mom, was, uh, the previous Pride leader? Because, you know . . ." Chloe trailed off.

That caused Kim to look up. She fixed Chloe with her eyes and closed her book.

"Your biological parents, whoever they were, are probably *dead.*"

Chloe jumped at the harshness of these words; while they were most likely true, they were spoken completely emotionlessly. It was like she had been slapped.

"You should worry about your *human* parents now, Chloe. They are alive. And they are probably being watched and probably in danger."

Chloe thought about the Tenth Bladers who'd caught her when she'd tried to go home. Home was a trap. They were expecting her to return home at some point. But what about her mom, the bait?

"Okay, chill," Chloe said, getting angry. She didn't even feel like pointing out how she only had *one* "human" parent. Was Kim acting all pissy because she'd never had any real family at all and was *jealous* of her? "I just want to know, all right? Who gave birth to me?"

"I will let you know as soon as Olga's people have found something," Kim said, opening her book again. The conversation was officially over.

Chloe left, still confused by the other girl's seeming animosity. Maybe it wasn't jealousy—maybe Kim, the one friend she had actually made since coming here, was now keeping her distance because of the danger surrounding Chloe. The thought only fueled Chloe to get out of Firebird. Now.

On the roof of the Sony Metreon, lying on her back and looking up at the sky, Chloe felt freer than she had in months. Thick clumps of gray clouds sped across the heavens like dumplings until they massed into a heavy blanket on the far eastern horizon. As they passed over the downtown area, they glowed orange from below, only regaining more natural shadows and sky colors as they headed out over the bay away from streetlights, neon signs, and other illuminating pollution.

She thought about how easy it would be just to run from rooftop to rooftop, never returning to the Mai, never returning to her school, and never returning home. Just living in the night. Not a street person . . . a *skyline* person, like Batman without his cave or his mansion. She could probably survive with her Mai abilities—heck, she knew how to run down a deer now. How hard would it be to steal something from a convenience store?

A lone figure came walking across the roof toward her. She didn't move; she could tell by his walk, sounds, and smells that it was Brian. He almost tripped over her, she was so black and still, blending in with the harsh shadows of the buildings.

He was perfect, like a vampire, his dark hair and eyes barely distinguishable against the night sky. The wind picked up and played with his hair a little, and he turned his head to look out at San Francisco. Chloe got a perfect view of his profile, from shadowed brow to bitten lips. A scarf waved behind him like the tattered cape of a worn-out superhero.

He lay down next to her, also looking up at the sky.

"Beautiful night," he observed. "Feels like a storm is coming."

"I want to run into it," Chloe said. "I want to run away."

Brian didn't say anything.

"I have everything I ever wanted. A father figure. A *rich* father figure," she added with a chuckle. "A family.

160

Being told, once and for all, that I really am *special*."

"I wish I was special," Brian said with a smile, quoting Radiohead. "You're so fucking special."

Chloe grinned sadly and sat up. She looked back down at him. The scarf that framed his head was soft chocolate brown and cashmere, knitted with intricate little cream diamonds in the pattern.

"You made this, didn't you?" she said, feeling the unbelievably downy ends and thinking about what had first brought them together, his funny homemade knit hat with the kitty cat ears.

"Yep. Had a lot of recent angst I needed to get out." He smiled ruefully. "You can always tell how upset I am by how crazy intricate the patterns are."

"You haven't . . . seen my mom, have you?" Chloe asked wistfully.

"No. My movements are kind of circumscribed these days. I got into a *load* of trouble after the whole bridge incident."

"Oh." She didn't say she was sorry. Chloe wasn't sure exactly what she did feel. An overwhelming sadness. A sense of loss or of having too much. "The Pride . . . I think it's like a cult."

There. She'd said it.

"Welcome to my world." Brian sighed, also sitting up. "You never hear the term used around the house, but there really is *no* line between 'cult' and certain 'secret orders'."

161

"Hey, you've got freckles," Chloe suddenly noticed, reaching over to touch his cheek. They were brown and added a lightheartedness to his features that wasn't normally there, without making him look too cute.

"I've been outside during the day a lot more recently. Since being, uh, dropped from your case. It's been kind of nice. I've been shadowing your friends some, making sure that they're okay, but it doesn't seem like either side is interested in them." He took her hand. "Thanks for trusting me, Chloe. For meeting me here. It means a lot to me."

"I'm beginning to think that no one's innocent of *anything*," Chloe answered with a lopsided smile. "But at least I think I know where you stand."

They were quiet for a moment. He didn't let go of her hand. She cuddled into him and looked up at the sky again. She thought about their first *real* date, when they'd gone to the zoo, and she'd bought him a stuffed monkey, and they'd talked about all sorts of important things.

"How did your mother die?" she asked softly.

Brian squeezed her hand and then dropped it. He played with some pebbles on the roof before answering. "My father's family has been in the Order since . . . well, since it was documented. All the way back to the *Mayflower* and England. Before that, actually. One time we were barons or princes or something in Italy. Royalty." Chloe could tell that he was being modest and knew exactly what they were and wasn't saying. "Italy . . .

Christendom . . . knights . . . the Crusades . . . I don't want to bore you with a history lesson.

"My mother's family comes from Klamath Falls, Oregon," he said with a smile. "My grandparents own a berry orchard.

"I guess like with any secret club, there are those who marry and *don't* tell their husbands and wives about it and those who marry and *do* tell their husbands and wives about it. But my father went beyond all that. He encouraged my mom to become a part of it *with* him.

"I don't think she really wanted to, but that may be my own subjective memory of it. I don't remember her getting involved much when I was little; I *do* remember her disappearing off with Dad later on, for long meetings and trips away, and practicing in the weapons room."

He threw a pebble down and stared at his empty hand. "She was killed on a mission. When I was twelve. They were raiding a Mai hideout in LA. She was shot in the head. Her face . . . It was a closed-casket funeral."

Chloe sucked in her breath. It explained a lot about Brian.

"One of . . ." What did she say? *Us? The Mai? Them?* "She was killed by a Mai?"

Brian laughed angrily. "That's what I thought for years. You've been living with them for a while now, Chloe. Have you ever seen someone with a weapon?"

She thought about the kizekh Ellen and Dmitri. She couldn't really remember what they carried.

163

"The Mai don't use guns," Brian hissed. "They almost never use any weapon with a blade, even. I didn't realize this; I mean I knew it, but I didn't put two and two together until a couple of years ago. My father let me believe it for *years*. . . . I finally found out the truth. She was killed by a random gang kid. He saw her gun, thought she was undercover or something, and let her have it."

Chloe shuddered. There were no clouds above at that moment, just a hazy sky with a few brave stars cutting through like diamond-tipped blades.

"She was killed for a cause she didn't even really believe in," Brian finished. "By someone who wasn't even involved."

Chloe struggled, looking for something to say. "Why did your father want her to join so much?"

"Because he's the head of the Order, Chloe."

A thousand things made sense now. Why Brian hated his dad. Why Brian, though he questioned and didn't approve of things the Order did, was still in it. He had been *raised* in the Order! It was all he had known his entire life. . . . Trying to leave it would be like Chloe leaving her mom and her friends and living an entirely new life, with new ideas and rules and people.

Yep. Exactly.

Chloe laughed quietly, a little crazily. Brian looked up at her, alarmed.

"My 'adoptive' father is the head of the Pride."

Brian blinked at her for a moment, then laughed himself.

"Great. Just *perfect*," he said. He put his arm around her and hugged her close to his side, a comforting gesture.

"Did you mean it before? On the phone?" Chloe asked softly. "Did you really mean you . . . ?"

"Yes." Brian closed his eyes, frowning. "I *love* you, Chloe." It was obviously hard for him to say, for a million different reasons. "Absolutely."

No one had ever said it to her before. Not outside of jokes, or out of friendship, or stupid grade school crushes. Not even Alyec; there was always humor around the word when he used it, like "love of my life", inflated, expressive, hyperbolic, and not really serious at all.

It made her giddy.

But how did *she* feel?

She didn't want to think about it right then. It might spoil the moment.

"But we can't—"

"Your lips are poison, Chloe," he said with a smile, knowing exactly how dramatic it sounded. "Your tears, your tongue, your saliva, your sweat . . . they would all kill me with extended contact."

Chloe leaned back, putting her head on his shoulder and his arms around her waist. Surely that was safe.

"We should go soon," he whispered in her ear, not quite touching it. She shivered at the feeling. "If we want to meet your friends on time."

" 'We'?"

"I'm not leaving you alone until you're by yourself

on the way home again. Your friends . . . They mean well, but they leave a trail as wide as the Grand Canyon." Chloe smiled, thinking of Amy and Paul trying to be stealthy. "Amy even found my e-mail address somehow. I told her to stay away, that it was all dangerous for them."

"She won't listen," Chloe said dreamily, pushing herself up against him more. She kissed his shoulder. "Let's just stay another minute or two?" she pleaded. "It's such a pretty night out. This is . . . *perfect*."

Brian opened his mouth to say something: that there were a thousand reasons why this wasn't perfect, starting with the fact that she was being hunted and ending with the fact that their relationship was ultimately doomed. But he swallowed whatever he was about to say.

"All right," he said, holding her more tightly. When she shivered, he took the scarf from around his neck and wrapped it around hers.

Chloe smiled and closed her eyes, but a single tear leaked out down her cheek.

She was supposed to meet Amy and Paul in the street behind Café Eland, private but close enough to the public where there couldn't be an attack. Brian kept assuring Chloe that the Order of the Tenth Blade would never hurt a human, that they took oaths to *protect* them, but Chloe only knew one thing: These days, wherever she went, trouble followed.

Brian shadowed her silently. She only heard or saw evidence of his presence once or twice along the way: a scuffed pebble in an alley, a shadow above. He was almost as adept at hiding as the Mai, and Chloe had the sneaking suspicion that the few times she thought she detected him, he was letting her.

She quickly checked out the coffee shop: 10:05, the back door was just swinging shut. In the summer the café put a couple of chairs out on the delivery dock in the back for its regular customers who knew they were there. Chloe scaled the fire escape of a building nearby and looked down.

Amy and Paul were there, Amy underdressed for the weather as always, stomping her feet, with her arms wrapped around some gigantic pink puffy coat that looked like it should be warm but obviously wasn't. Paul was looking around, a drink in one hand and a cigarette in the other, nervously tapping ashes onto the pavement below.

Something pulled inside Chloe, seeing her two friends from above. It was like in a book: she was apart, beyond them, not part of their story and lives. Before she could think any more along those lines, she dropped down neatly out of the sky in front of them.

"Holy *shit*," Paul said. Chloe was gratified to see that he was actually capable of losing his cool: half of his hot chocolate went flying.

"Chloe!" Amy shrieked. Both Paul and Chloe gave

her looks. "I mean, *Chloe!*" she whispered, then threw her arms around her friend.

"Hey," Chloe said weakly, the air being pushed out of her. Paul ruffled her hair.

"What the hell, King," he said, his voice thick with barely contained emotion. "Where have you been?"

"And what are you *wearing?*" Amy asked, looking at the expensive jeans and long-sleeved black tee with *Paris* in gold grommets across it, the mismatched but beautiful scarf.

"Someone else's stuff." Chloe hopped back up on the rail that cordoned off the delivery area. The move was as smooth and graceful and impossible as when she'd landed in front of them.

"Uh," Paul said, clearing his throat, not sure what else to say.

"It's a long story. I only have a few minutes. Anybody get me a coffee?"

Amy managed to pull a venti out of one of the pockets in her pink coat; it hadn't spilled at all. Chloe took it, slipped down from the rail, and slugged back several swallows gratefully. "Russians," she began, "like really sweet and disgusting drinks."

Then Chloe took a deep breath. There really was no simple way to say it.

"Okay. Here goes. My people, the Mai, are actually an ancient race of cat warriors. The Order of the Tenth Blade is a Knights-Templar-style organization that has been trying to wipe them out for the last five thousand years or so."

Amy and Paul just looked at her.

"There is no Russian Mafia," Chloe went on. "At least, not in this case. It's a race war."

"Okay . . . ," Amy said carefully, trying not to look around her to see if other people heard.

"I believe you," Paul said in a tone that meant exactly the opposite.

Chloe knew her friends well enough to be pretty sure that they were trying to figure out the fastest, quietest way to get her to the psych ward at a hospital.

Chloe sighed and held up her hand.

"Okay, does *this* convince you?"

With a whisper-soft *sslting* noise, she extended her claws.

"Mother*fuck*," Amy said, eyes widening like those of an anime character.

Paul grabbed Chloe's hand and looked closely at the base of her claws, feeling around the tips of her fingers for prosthetics or a glove or something.

"I have foot claws, too," Chloe said casually, trying not to laugh at their reactions. "And I think my eyes go all slitty—like diamonds—when I'm in the dark. I can see at night, you know."

"I don't believe . . . ," Paul said, not dropping her hand.

"Believe," Chloe suggested sweetly. She pulled away from him and leapt straight up so that she landed standing on the rail. Then she bent over and stood on her hands, using her claws to clasp the metal. She did a couple of backflips.

"Okay, the über-nails thing I could question," Amy finally said. "But the Chloe King *I* know could barely touch her toes."

"This is completely fucked up," Paul muttered with grudging admiration. "You're just like Wolverine. It's so unfair. *I* read comic books and *you* get the superpowers."

Chloe sat down, took another slug of coffee, and told them *everything*. Starting from the personal: the night she beat up the mugger to the night Alyec took her to the Mai, with extra details on what happened after her friends left. "I *knew* we shouldn't have abandoned you," Amy said, hands on her hips. Then Chloe moved on to the historic and impersonal: as much as she knew about the Order of the Tenth Blade and the Mai and the history of the Mai (with many mental apologies to the book of the same name she'd never finished).

And she finally told the truth—all of the truths—about Alyec and Brian.

"I wish *I* had claws," Amy said wistfully, running her fingers over them. "It's like . . . your own personal defense system. You could go *any*where by yourself at night and not have to worry about rapists or muggers or anything."

"No," Chloe agreed, "only an entire organization whose sole purpose is to wipe out people like me."

"That's why they . . . your *Mai* . . . won't let you out to see us?"

"Yeah, I tried to sneak out to see my mom a couple

of weeks ago and was completely ambushed. I would have died if some of the kizekh hadn't been trailing me." Of course, now that she thought about it, she remembered that the man in the sweater had had handcuffs, not a garrote or daggers like the Rogue. Still, his intentions were obviously not good.

"So why don't they just send you out with a group of them in the open?" Paul asked suspiciously.

"They have to keep a low profile."

"Yeah? Or do they just want to cut you off from your past life? With your human friends and family?"

"They just want to keep me safe," Chloe said uncertainly. The words that came out of her friends' mouths were suspiciously similar to the ideas that had been forming in the back of her own head, in the murky area where the word *cult* had first caught her attention.

"It sounds like it all kind of sucks." Amy sighed. "But I *still* want claws. Was this the reason you wanted a manicure that day?"

"Sort of."

She told them about Xavier. How the night she'd fallen from the tower, she'd hooked up with a random guy and as a result, he'd almost died from where she'd clawed him on the back in the heat of passion. For some reason, it was far more difficult to talk about this to her two best friends than anything else. It was just sort of embarrassing. "So we can't, like, have sex or *do* anything with normal humans, 'cause it kills them."

"That doesn't make any sense," Paul said, thinking about it. "I'm sure you must have kissed someone, like in grade school, at a party, or as a joke or something."

Chloe shrugged. "It has to do with the spit itself, I guess. A peck on the cheek doesn't do anything. It's more like tongue to tongue. It just started around when, well"—Chloe shot an apologetic look at Paul—"I finally got my period. It's all about puberty, I guess."

Paul looked deeply uncomfortable, though he tried his best to hide it.

"And your mom doesn't know *any* of this?" Amy asked, amazed.

Chloe shrugged. "This has all been kinda recent, and it's all kinda hard to believe. I was thinking about maybe trying to sneak over to see my mom tonight after you guys," Chloe went on dully. "But smarter than last time. Not just, like, walking up to the front door."

"Oh. Uh." Amy and Paul exchanged another look. Paul cleared his throat again. "That's another reason we wanted to see you, Chloe."

"I think your mom's missing," Amy blurted. "I broke into your house about a week ago and it was like no one had been there for a while."

Chloe stared at her, mind numb.

"We were going to call the police," Paul began.

"I have to go home," Chloe whispered, and then, without another word, she turned and ran.

"Wait! Chloe!" Amy called out to the figure disappearing into the night.

"Chloe!" came a new voice, masculine, from somewhere above them. "Chloe! Don't go! It's a trap! Chloe . . . !"

Paul and Amy looked at each other, then ran after their friend.

Chloe ran until her lungs shrieked from the cold air and lack of oxygen, until her insides stung with heart attack pain. Even with her Mai strength and speed, she was pushing herself far harder than she ever had. When a car blocked her way, she leapt, sinking her hand claws into its roof and pulling herself over it like a pole vaulter, leaving the driver with a horrible tearing sound in his ears and the image of rabid dogs and werewolf movies in his mind. She stuck to the streets and lower levels, not wanting to waste any time with the sort of stunts she usually enjoyed on her nighttime runs. She felt her foot claws trying to come out, straining at the fabric in her sneakers. On one landing, they finally pushed through the soles of her Sauconys, grabbing the dirt below her to push her forward.

Chloe ignored the shadows around her. She was far too fast a moving target this time to worry about an ambush. She was only concentrating on one thing: the nightmare that had kept her awake since the whole thing began. Bringing the violence that was now part of her life home, onto her mom.

She ran up the steps and unlocked the door, slamming it open, and threw herself in.

"Mom?" she called.

A step in and she instantly knew something was wrong.

The air *was* stale, as Amy had suggested; there were no recent human movements, warmth, or smells in there except for her friend's. None of her mom's perfume, soap, or skin scent was less than a week old. And there was a rancid, rotting scent beneath everything, like the drain in the sink hadn't been cleaned in a while.

Chloe flipped on the lights. Everything looked exactly the same as it had the last afternoon she'd been there, except for a few glasses that were put near the sink. Maybe when her mom had come home from work and found that note of Chloe's—she looked around frantically. There it was, by the phone. Scribbled in her mom's handwriting on it was Keira's number under her name; Mrs. King had fully intended on checking up to see if her daughter really was where she said she was.

Hummus. Chloe realized what the sour smell was. She followed it to the fridge, where a clump of it trailed down the outside of the door. It was so unlike neat freak Anna King that Chloe felt her heart stop when she saw it. She opened the door and saw the open container of hummus, now molding.

On its surface, the word *help* had been sloppily inscribed.

Nineteen

I can't believe this.

The first coherent thoughts Anna King was able to form as the drug wore off were incredulous and disbelieving. She opened her eyes to confirm what she was *sure* couldn't be true.

She was tied to a chair. Just like out of the movies, she had come to, tied to a chair.

It was a very comfortable chair, more like a La-Z-Boy or lounger, and she wasn't tied to it *exactly* like in the movies, but still. Her arms were belted onto the tops of the armrests—the chair had been neatly altered specifically for this purpose. Her feet were connected to each other by some sort of hobble, rendering it impossible for her to walk, much less get up, but that did not prevent her from being able to switch to more comfortable sitting positions.

She closed her eyes again, still sluggish and sleepy.

The drug was thick in her mouth, like a morning-after-Nyquil hangover but a thousand times worse. They'd given it to her after they'd slipped her out of the house. As soon as she opened the door, she knew something suspicious was up. Years of living in the city first by herself, and then later as a single mom, had made her sensitive to vibes. They were polite and the woman in the group had asked if they could come in. When Anna had said no, they'd somehow wound up inside anyway. She'd pretended she wasn't scared, putting pieces of dinner away. They talked about her daughter, and the trouble Chloe might be in, and how they wanted to help. She'd written the word *help* in the hummus, inspired and terrified.

It was a good thing she'd done that, too, since a few minutes later she was trying to scream and they had a gag over her mouth and there was a big, sleek car like out of the movies and she was taken away into darkness.

"Mrs. King," someone was saying gently, trying to wake her up more.

"Anna," she corrected instantly, in lawyer mode. She blinked a few times before managing to keep her eyes open. Someone had thoughtfully taken her glasses when they kidnapped her and had put them on her when she was passed out.

The room came into focus after a couple of moments of blurriness. She was in an office or a library, nicely appointed with a thick wool rug and big mahogany desk. A man was leaning back on it, almost sitting, legs crossed. He was a large man, middle-aged and white, with a sleek patience in his eyes that Anna the lawyer instantly recognized as a direct result of having money and/or power. He was dressed in a suit without the jacket, his tie loosened.

"How are you feeling?" he asked politely.

She opened her mouth to tell him precisely how she was feeling, but nothing came out, like she had used up all her speech with her name before. *"Water,"* was all she managed to croak instead.

"Of course." He turned to look at someone blocked from her view by the side of her chair—she had begun to think of it as *her* chair—and made a little motion with his hands. Quiet footsteps went off to do his bidding, no questions asked. Money *and* power, she decided.

A moment later someone handed him a glass of ice water. He came forward, and just when Anna was afraid he was going to *feed* her, he unlatched her left arm and let her take the glass herself. She didn't drain it instantly; this was not a time to show weakness. Instead she took polite, demure little sips, as though she were at a dinner party.

"Is that better?" the man asked.

"Where's my daughter?" she countered.

"What?" the man said with wry amusement. "You don't think she's at her friend Keira's house?"

"What have you done with my daughter?" Anna repeated.

177

"*We* haven't done anything, Anna. Although Chloe *is* in a lot of trouble—she has fallen in with a bad crowd and has been involved in a murder."

The doubt that flashed through Anna King's mind registered nowhere on her face. "I don't think so," she said.

"Well, I'm afraid she has." The man sighed, crossing his arms. "One of my friends—one of my colleagues—is dead because of her."

"You keep *not* saying that she killed him," Anna noted, sounding exactly like the attorney that she was. "'Involved in a murder' and 'dead because of.'"

The man laughed, and his full, jowly chin shook a little. His voice was rich and beautiful, and every time he used it, Chloe's mother hated him more. "You are absolutely correct, of course; this is not a black-and-white world. We have no actual proof that my friend is dead."

"Why am I here," Anna said wearily, "and where is Chloe?"

"Chloe is with her new friends, most likely. To make a long story as short as possible, Mrs. Ki—*Anna*—your daughter's biological family is from a long line of . . . well, I guess you could call them warriors of a sort, or maybe a hunting caste—more than anachronistic in this day and age. Anyway, her people want her back. We have reason to believe they contacted her about a month ago and are fairly certain she is with them now."

Anna stared at him for a long moment before speaking. Even though she was the one tied to a chair, with her blondish hair coming out in wisps around her cockeyed glasses, she didn't feel like *she* was the ridiculous one in the room.

"Do you mean to tell me that some crazy ancient Russian Mafia wants Chloe to join them like her parents did?"

"Something like that, yes."

"If you care so very much about my daughter's welfare, why aren't you talking to the police or to me on the phone instead of kidnapping me and tying me to a chair?"

"Well, that brings us to your first question, doesn't it?" The man uncrossed his legs and put his arms behind him, supporting himself on the desk. "*You* are here because the Mai are extremely dangerous. In situations that have occurred before, with adoptive children of American parents, they have been known to kill the parents to ensure complete loyalty of the child and to cut off all connections with the rest of the world."

"And again, why do you care?"

"The Mai don't play by normal rules—they are like a gang, but far worse. Very much like the mob you mentioned. My organization exists to protect the public from them. To limit their influence. Hopefully one day to destroy them completely."

"How charitable of you."

"My wife was killed trying to save someone from the

Mai," he said softly. "I don't want you or anyone else suffering the same fate."

Both were silent for a moment. The corners of the room were obscured in gloom, and there were no windows. She was someplace secret, dark, and impossible to find. Mrs. King felt like squirming, both from his gaze and from sitting still for so long, never mind how comfortable the chair was. She didn't, though. "Why am I"—she pulled at her right arm—"still tied to the chair if you're just trying to protect me?"

"Anna, if we had come to your house and told you what I just did, would you have come quietly along with us?"

He did have a point.

"It was imperative to get you out of your house *as soon as possible*, as quietly as possible. Any one of a number of things may happen next—someone, a hit man from the Mai, may be sent in to kill you—or Chloe herself might try to sneak out and visit you, encouraging them to have you killed, even if they hadn't decided to before. Remember, they want complete control of their members' lives. I'm sorry about any unpleasantness, but this really was the easiest way. Now we can keep you safe while seeing what can be done about Chloe."

"Will you release me?"

"Yes—but I'm afraid we're going to have to keep you confined for a time. In a much nicer room than this," he added quickly and apologetically. "The temptation for you to leave and try to find your daughter would be far too great."

So let me get this straight. The "good guys" are holding me captive so I can't get hurt seeing my daughter, who is being held captive by the bad guys who don't want her out seeing her mother.

"What *is* going to happen to Chloe? Can you"—*save* sounded too melodramatic—"get her?"

"Of course." But there was something in his face, a slightly surprised look, as though he had already dismissed Chloe and her fate. As though Anna herself and *her* safety were all that mattered now. *He probably considers her one of "them" now. Chloe will get no help here.*

"Who *are* you people?" she demanded, half sarcastically.

"I'm afraid I—"

"Can't tell me that either. Yeah, of course."

"You can call me Whit," the man offered.

Anna had every intention of escaping as soon as she saw a way. She might not return home; she agreed with her captor that would be a pretty dangerous thing to do. But she *would* go immediately to the police and call the cult hotline and tell them about *everyone*.

Twenty

Chloe was still sitting on the floor, head in her hands, when Brian came in.

"It's all my fault," she said miserably.

He knelt down and she buried her face in his shoulder. "It is *not* your fault."

She shook her head, trying to wipe the tears away.

"We should leave here soon," Brian said as calmly as he could. "I gave the members of the Order who were patrolling here false tips that you were seen at Pateena's. But it's only going to be a few minutes before they get there and figure out that it was a trick." She nodded and sniffed. He stood up and looked around. "Are you *sure* she's gone?"

Chloe nodded again, wiping her face and pointing to the bowl of hummus.

"O . . . kay . . . ," Brian said, raising his eyebrows. "Your mom is certainly a . . . resourceful woman."

Chloe tried to smile. She felt embarrassingly weak,

like a child who needed to be taken care of in a time of crisis, and here was savior Brian, rushing in to fulfill the role of hero. But she needed that right now.

"Ohmygod Chloe." Amy burst through the door, wheezing, bent over. Her hair was frizzing around her face like a solar flare, and several strands were plastered to her face with sweat. "Youreneversupposedtoreturn-tothesceneof—" She took a deep breath and noticed Brian. "Who the hell is *that*?"

"This is Brian. Brian, Amy," Chloe introduced formally, feeling a little ridiculous.

"*This* is Brian?" her friend said incredulously. She looked him over, up and down so carefully that he began to fidget under her gaze. "You are *way* hotter than Alyec."

Chloe shook her head with impatience. "Where's Paul?"

"He's coming. The, uh, you know"—she mimicked taking a drag from a cigarette—"slow him down."

"That and managing to skip every gym class since the dawn of time," Chloe muttered. Now was not the time to have people separated. The Tenth Blade "patrols" might have let them pass for now, but what if they were just waiting for more orders? And what if the Mai noticed she was missing and thought Brian was trying to abduct her? "We've got to find my mom."

"Absolutely," Amy agreed, still panting. "Where do you think she went?"

"Now, wait a moment . . . ," Brian began, putting his hand up to Chloe's friend.

"I don't think she *went* anywhere. I think she was taken." Chloe pointed to the bowl.

"Hey." Paul came in, trying not to huff, his face turning red as a result. For the first time ever, he actually looked healthy, with pink cheeks.

"*This* is Brian," Amy said, grabbing Paul's arm.

"Hey," Paul said again, waving and still trying to breathe normally. It was amazing, Chloe reflected. His clothes were still perfect. Of course, Puma originally made athletic gear, but still . . .

"Chloe's mom has definitely been kidnapped," Amy said, catching him up on things. "We're working out how to find her."

"*We* aren't doing any such thing," Brian said, exasperated. Suddenly he seemed a lot more than just a couple of years older than Chloe and her friends. "*You two* are now officially done with this part of the story. I thought I made that clear in my answer to that e-mail you so unwisely sent me."

"Oh, suddenly Mr. Studmuffin here is charge of everything," Amy snapped, putting her hands on her hips and sticking her chin out at him. "Where the hell did you come from, anyway? '*We two*' have been friends with her forever."

"I appreciate that," Brian said through clenched teeth, "but this is very. Dangerous. Stuff. Your friend has been involved in what might be considered a murder. A group of people are out for her blood. Another group of people are out to protect her at all costs. And now her mom is gone. Hello? Not the safest avenue for you two."

"I'm right *here*, people," Chloe muttered.

"What makes *you* so qualified for the role of detective and bodyguard?" Amy had come closer to Brian and, even though she was a head shorter, pressed her nose up as far as it would go. Paul was still trying to catch his breath, watching without saying anything.

"He is . . . was . . . is?" Chloe said, looking at Brian uncertainly. "A member of the Order of the Tenth Blade."

"The kooks who are trying to kill you?" Paul asked, amazed, finally able to speak.

"Yeah, but he saved me on the bridge. . . ."

"How do you know he's not a double agent or something?" Amy demanded.

"I'm not," Brian said.

"I don't," Chloe added.

"He doesn't seem like it," Paul offered.

"Well, *you've* taken a sudden switch," Amy said, rounding on her boyfriend. "I thought *Alyec* was the one you trusted."

"Okay, everyone, *stop*," Chloe finally said. Brian obviously knew what he was doing and had a pretty good idea of what was best for everyone, but it was also crystal clear that her friends weren't going to listen to him. "Arguing here, the four of us, from three different factions, isn't going to help anything. And it's just keeping all of us nice and neatly in the same spot for *someone* to come along and pick off."

"What faction are we?" Paul asked.

"Innocent," Chloe said, gritting her teeth. Amy started to say something, but Chloe interrupted her. "No, shut up, it's true. There's no reason to put your lives in danger. But from what I understand, the Tenth Blade won't hurt humans, and I don't think the Mai like attracting too much attention to themselves. You're in a perfect position to help on the detective side. Like the home base people." Amy and Paul looked at her blankly. "Like Oracle in *Batman*," she said desperately. "Like Willow in *Buffy*. Before the whole witch-powers thing. Like Pete in *Smallville*."

"Oh, cool," Paul said, relaxing and suddenly looking into it. Amy looked doubtful but nodded.

It is kind of a lame-ass cop-out, Chloe realized, but she hoped it sounded good and that her friends would accept it. She wasn't going to be responsible for more people she loved getting hurt because of her.

"We can do other things," Amy protested weakly.

"You aren't trained like the Order, and you don't have the abilities of the Mai," Brian pointed out. "If you got involved in an actual fight, you'd be seriously injured or killed. I hate to sound clichéd, but this isn't a game."

"Do a search of all of the newspapers for the last two

weeks," Chloe suggested quickly before Amy yelled at Brian again. *He has such a habit of coming off as well meaning but a little high and mighty.* She wondered if his father was like that and, if so, how he managed to retain control of his organization. "We need to see if there's anything, *anything* about a missing person, a body, someone in the hospital. . . ." She didn't *say* "the morgue," but Chloe could tell by the look on Amy's face that it was understood.

"Do we have any *idea* who kidnapped her?" Paul asked.

Chloe looked at Brian helplessly.

"It could be either the Mai or the Order at this point," he answered, shrugging. "Both have a motive."

"Why would it be the Mai?" Chloe demanded. "What would they want with my mother?"

"Chloe, she's your biggest connection to the world of humans." Brian *knew* this was a touchy thing to say in front of her two best friends, but he had to say it anyway. "If they thought you would completely go over to their side—"

"What do you mean, *over*? I live with them—they're my race and my family and want to get to know me and protect me from people—*humans*—who want to kill me!"

"I'm just saying we should keep it open as a possibility," Brian said as calmly as he could. "As you said, they are extremely *protective* of their race."

"But what you're saying still doesn't make sense,

Brian," Amy said unexpectedly, before Chloe could speak. "The Mai have no reason to *take* Mrs. King. What would they do with her? Why not just"—she glanced at Chloe, having a hard time saying it—"why not just have her turn up dead on the news? Then Chloe would have nowhere to turn, and she would have to stay with them."

"They would never do that," Chloe said slowly. "And they may want me to stay, but they've been nothing besides supportive and—" She didn't know what to call it.

There was something about having a guy like a father play chess with her and eat pizza, about having a group of people who she could just lounge with instantly accept her, not act pissed off or angry—or date her other best friend. They accepted her without conditions. Once she'd appeared, she was just there, part of the Mai, like she had always been and always would be.

Plus—and here was the bit she wasn't going to reveal to anyone present yet—the Mai made *perfect* bloodhounds. As soon as she got back, she planned on telling Sergei about what had happened. Even if he was reluctant, Chloe bet she could wheedle a couple of kizekh out of him to help track down her mom. And deal with her captors, if necessary.

"All right . . . ," Paul said, obviously not entirely convinced, but enough to not press it. Brian's face was carefully neutral. "She hasn't turned up dead yet, and whatever this was, it happened a while ago. But . . ." he

189

paused. "There doesn't seem to be a logical reason for *either* side to delay your finding out about it. Is there anyone else we should know about? Someone else who might have taken your mother for some different reason? Who might not have anything to do with any of this at all?"

"Yeah, sure," Amy said, making a face. "Because *two* obvious secret organizations with hidden agendas aren't convincing enough for you, Paul?"

"Well, I mean, what if it was someone else close to you, Chloe—another interested party, with a totally different *x* factor?" Paul suggested.

"Like *who*?"

Amy's eyes suddenly widened with realization of who fit the bill perfectly. "Like . . . your dad, Chloe?"

"No way." Paul shook his head. "That's not what I meant at all. Why would he come back after all these years and do something like this? I don't remember him being that kind of psycho—and my parents don't talk about him that way."

"Yeah, I'm afraid I'm going to have to vote negatory on that, too, Ames," Chloe said, physically shaking her head free of all the different theories. She checked her cell phone. "Okay, look, I gotta go. I'm going to have to keep this off—it's got *no* juice left."

"Now, that's something I *can* help you with," Amy said, grinning. She dug into her enormous pink coat pocket and triumphantly pulled out a rugged but shiny techno-gadget. "And it has a charger. Here." She handed that over, too.

"What are you, Q from *James Bond*?" Chloe asked. "What *is* this?"

"A walkie-talkie," Amy explained proudly. "We've got one, too. Keep it on, and we'll always be in contact—untraceably."

"Wow. This must have been expensive. . . ."

"That's a nice model," Brian said approvingly, looking over her shoulder. "It's a newer one than my dad sells. Hey, doesn't it have—?"

Paul kicked him. Chloe blushed, wondering how much it must have cost her friends.

"Thanks, guys," she said, trying not to cry again. "You really *are* my support team. Even if," she added, with a grin at Amy, "you dress like a pimp."

Twenty-one

Chloe made Brian stop following her after they got to the other side of the bridge, not wanting to lead him to Sergei's house—although the way he didn't question where she'd gone made her wonder if maybe the Order of the Tenth Blade knew more about the Mai and their whereabouts than they were letting on. But Brian was a man of his word, and even though she paused often to scent the wind and listen for his footsteps, she found no trace of him. At one point she ran back and trailed *him* to see if her senses were correct, and they were: he had wandered back over the bridge. He'd stopped halfway across and looked back, maybe hoping for a sign of her. Finally he stuck his hands in his pockets and continued the rest of the way hunched over, looking at the ground. Not a silent, highly trained soldier of an elite order, but rather a failing hero—as though nothing good was going to happen if he wasn't there to protect her.

Something burned in the pit of her stomach when

she saw him like that. Chloe had to fight back an almost overwhelming urge to chase back after him and grab him. She could just see it: *He would hug her and lift her high off the ground. And when he put her down, he'd put his hand under her chin and kiss her*—But that was when the dream broke off.

That could never happen. That *would* never happen.

But watching him walk away from her toward San Francisco, she knew he could never be just a friend, either.

I love you, Chloe.

She let herself savor Brian's words one more time before heading back to Sergei's house.

Sergei was in his office with Igor, Olga, and some of the other higher-ranking Mai at Firebird.

"Sergei?" Chloe flashed an apologetic look to everyone else in the room, but it wasn't really heartfelt.

"Hello, Chloe," he said amicably. "We're a *little* busy right now. . . ."

"My mom is gone."

Everyone on the other side of the desk shifted and looked at each other in surprise. Sergei raised his eyebrows.

"I snuck out," Chloe said, coming farther into the room. She was slightly ashamed, but honesty really was the best policy in this case. Here was an army of people already on her side who could help her, trained with techniques and abilities specifically geared toward hunting and finding people. "I went to go see my friends,

Amy and Paul—they were worried about me." She tried not to look at Sergei's face, terrified of the disappointment she might find there. "They told me they thought she might be missing—our house didn't seem lived in, and she wasn't answering phone calls. So I went home—" There were some sharp intakes of breath from everyone around her. "She's obviously been taken, or kidnapped, or something. Days ago. Maybe right after I came here."

There were murmurs and low discussions. Olga gave her a sad look. Sergei bit his lip.

"I'm very sorry, Chloe." He sounded sad, but not surprised.

"We've got to *do* something," Chloe said, trying to ignore the sound of resignation she heard in his voice. "She might not be dead yet—we could track down whoever has her . . . like a hunt. . . ." She trailed off.

"I'm afraid we can't do that." Sergei looked down at his desk, as if he'd been expecting her to ask that, or this was the answer he had been forced to give others before. "Call the police if you want from one of our private phones, tip them off. But we cannot get involved."

"But this is my *mom*," Chloe said, desperately trying to think of some way of convincing him, of some point that he would accede to. "She raised me—and kept me safe until you found me."

"Chloe, we all feel terrible about this," Sergei said with feeling. "But I cannot risk the dwindling kizekh on such a mission. There are few enough of them as it is to protect *us*. And as for a *hunt* in the city—we cannot face that sort of exposure. *Ever.* The Order of the Tenth Blade would love nothing more than to see us out and around San Francisco; it would give them the excuse they need to attack in heavier forces. Not to mention if the police took notice. No, I'm sorry, Chloe, we cannot risk such a thing. Especially for a human."

The businesslike attitude with which he closed the discussion jarred Chloe even more than what he'd said.

"But this human . . . is my *mother*. . . ." She tried not to cry.

"I'm sorry, Chloe," he said again, a little more kindly. "There are so few of us. It is terrible that we have to so selfishly look to our own survival, but I'm afraid that is the way it is."

Chloe looked to the other Mai in the room, but most looked away or down at the floor. Only Olga met her gaze, with a sympathetic sadness.

Chloe thought about saying something sarcastic and final, about how they weren't a *real* true family, but realized that if she opened her mouth or even stayed half a second longer, she would begin to cry. She turned to leave, trying not to run.

Sergei sighed loudly behind her. "Someone have Ellen and Dmitri follow her again. She's going to look for trouble."

★   ★   ★

But she *didn't* go looking for trouble immediately.

First she called the Ilychovich household and left a message; that was all she could do—as far as she knew, Alyec didn't have a cell phone, and she should know, right? Then she wandered around aimlessly for a while, trying not to check her voice mail too often, miserably wishing he would somehow know to call or show up. She finally wound up in the library, which was dark, empty, and quiet; good for thinking. Chloe made her way over to a window seat and tucked herself up in it, looking outside.

It was a beautiful, surreally bright night, like something out of a painting or Narnia. The sky was a deep, rich blue, the moon a silver, detailed orb of shining white that made perfect beams when Chloe looked at it through her eyelashes. The great emerald lawn was a rich shade of black.

Chloe hadn't been outside in daylight for weeks, but it felt much longer—like a lifetime. She felt a strange, removed feeling. It reminded her of the clinking of glasses as her mom cleaned up dinner, like there was some order to the world that she wasn't quite part of. She couldn't help feeling a little stupid. Life wasn't like TV, and she had definitely *not* been whisked away to her Happily Ever After. No one could do that, she realized. Not even an ancient, hidden race of people with powers like lions who gathered in prides.

There were no real superheroes.

Why had she assumed that just because they had

these abilities, they would automatically come to the aid of the weak, defenseless, and—most of all—*innocent?* Rationally, she understood Sergei's reasons: there wasn't a huge population of Mai to begin with. Like pandas. Losing even one panda was a problem, too.

But forget helping to rescue her mom just for the sake of doing good; Sergei wouldn't do it for *her.* Didn't he . . . well, if he didn't *love* her, didn't he care about her? Didn't he care about saving the woman who was responsible for keeping Chloe—one of their kind—safe until she could join them? Couldn't he do Chloe this one favor?

The moon slowly glided across the sky, inching toward midnight, and Chloe watched the intricate shadows in the grass grow and change direction.

She was still at the window hours later when Kim came padding in, carrying a sheaf of papers and clippings and photographs. She wore a long black turtleneck sweater and a black skirt that went to the floor, making her look like an ancient priestess. A cat-eared female—and, Chloe noted wryly—a pretty sexy priestess.

"I have some pictures for you. Your relatives . . . I mean, they might be."

"I thought you didn't want to talk about it."

Kim sighed patiently, as if she had expected this response but didn't feel the need to apologize.

"How did you know I was here?"

Kim blinked once, then touched her nose.

"Of course." Chloe looked back out the window. "My mom's gone. You were right about my 'human parents' being in danger."

"I'm . . . sorry that I was right."

"Sergei and Olga and the others . . . they won't *do* anything. They won't help me. They won't risk the kizekh. . . ." She pounded her fist on the window sash. "And what can *I* do? If I try to go out, Sergei's goons will drag me back to make sure I'm 'safe.' If I manage to *get* out—and get anywhere near my home without an army, the Tenth Bladers will get me. . . ." She trailed off. "I guess I'll call the police, like Sergei said. It's the only thing I really can do."

"I'll help," Kim said simply.

"What?" Chloe looked at her; she hadn't really been talking *to* the other girl, just getting her thoughts out.

"I'll help. I'm the best tracker here anyway. We will return to the scene of the crime and look for clues." She said this in such even tones that Chloe worried she was joking. Not that Kim had a great sense of humor or anything.

"Really?" Chloe asked slowly.

Kim nodded. "I can evade the goons, too. So, do you want to see these pictures?"

It was like the conversation was over as far was Kim was concerned. She had made her choice, and that was that. Chloe stared at her a little more.

"I'm totally thrilled, but I have to ask—why are you helping me?"

"You're my friend," Kim said, shrugging. "And I believe that once you tell him, Alyec will come along, too. Unlike him, however, I will not be expecting physical rewards from you."

Chloe suddenly exploded with laughter—like she hadn't since Alyec had teased her into a good mood in the middle of the school hall. That felt like it has been ages ago. Her face relaxed into a smile. It felt good.

She held her hand out for the photos. "Let's see these."

"That woman in the background—and clearer, here: she is the former pride leader. The one who *might* be your mother."

Chloe took the picture from her. It was cracked and bent and had what looked like coffee rings in a corner. The woman in it was certainly not as pretty as Chloe, but there was a definite resemblance, with the high cheekbones and cupid's bow lips. Her eyes were also hazel but darker, or at least they seemed shadowed in the picture. Her forehead was wider. She was handsome and had thick black hair that came down over her shoulders and covered her breasts. She was laughing, and her whole body was involved: her head thrown back, her hands on her hips, her mouth wide open, exposing perfect white teeth. There were deep creases around her eyes, like she had seen more of the world than her age would seem to indicate.

"Both my moms spent their lives helping people," Chloe murmured.

"What do you mean?"

"My mother—my human mother—is a lawyer in a private firm, but she does a lot of work for legal aid. Mainly for a women's domestic abuse shelter in the Mission District."

"She sounds like a good person."

"She is." Chloe smiled weakly. "Thanks for not saying 'was.'"

Kim just blinked at her. Chloe wondered how much of the girl's slow transformation to something more cat than human had affected her mind.

"How did you know my mom might be in danger?" Chloe asked aloud.

Once again Kim looked uncomfortable. "It only stands to reason," she said slowly. "For one thing, she makes perfect bait for the Tenth Bladers to lure you out."

"And . . . ?"

"And if you are still asking the question, you are already familiar with the other possible answer." She bit the sentence off as she finished it. Chloe knew she wouldn't get more out of her about it. She continued flipping through the pictures.

"My friend Amy suggested that it might not have anything to do with the Mai or the Order of the Tenth Blade," she added casually. "My dad left when I was really young—my mom's story is that he went gradually psycho or something. It wasn't exactly an amicable breakup."

"I . . . don't think he's a likely suspect. Occam's Razor—the simplest explanation is usually the correct one."

"Yeah, that's what I think, too," Chloe said, sighing. "But it was kind of exciting thinking about him for a little while again, you know? I wonder what he's doing now. . . ." She shook her head. "I didn't know him very well. As a kid I thought he was a superhero, the best dad ever . . . and then an asshole for walking out on us. Of course, for a long time I blamed my mom for that." Chloe frowned, thinking about the fight they'd had the night she discovered her claws. "Then it turns out that one of the reasons they split up was because of *me*. . . . They had very different ideas on child raising. Apparently he was this super-strict jerk, all about not letting me go out or date or—" She stopped and looked away from the photos to Kim. "*Not letting me go*—he made my mom promise before he took off. To not let me date."

Kim came to the same conclusion she had. "Did your parents know what you are?"

"My mom doesn't," Chloe said, pretty sure of the fact. Things like claws and litter boxes had not been brought up during the tampons and Advil discussion. "But what if my father knew?"

"Then your mother's disappearance becomes even more complex. Aside from the Tenth Blade, I think I can say with some certainty that almost no humans know about us."

"It would be on the news instantly," Chloe agreed.

"Perhaps he was Mai," Kim wondered.

"Um, no? The whole sex thing? She'd be all, like, dead and stuff?"

"Oh. Of course," Kim said, blushing. She turned back to the manila envelope in her hand. "So you had no father growing up . . . ," the girl said, playing with the idea. "I can see why you would get attached to Sergei so quickly."

"What's *that* supposed to mean?" Chloe snapped.

"Nothing more than that he is a charismatic, charming, and powerful leader. A perfect father figure. A role he enjoys, I might add. There have been other . . . orphans he has attached himself to."

Was Kim trying to make her jealous? But that didn't make sense unless *she* was one of those other orphans, who'd maybe gotten dumped when Chloe or someone else came along. Like Igor. He certainly looked to Sergei as a male role model. Maybe it was a warning?

"Did he take *you* under his wing?"

"Yes," Kim said hesitantly, "when I first came."

"What happened? You don't seem to like him very much."

"That was it. I never have." Kim shrugged. "There is very little room for personal choice among the Mai, especially if you're an orphan, being welcomed in by the only people who will—who *can*—take you. But something about him . . . I didn't like him from the beginning. So I was raised by everyone and no one."

Chloe thought about this, drumming her fingers on the photos. There was a lot of information in what the other girl had just told her, but she wasn't quite sure what to do with it yet. So Sergei liked to take the lonely under his wing—what was wrong with that? It was *nice*, in a sort of den-mother-at-the-orphanage kind of way. And Kim *was* kind of a freak—maybe she just resented authority figures. Maybe this was nothing more than a slight personality clash of two very different people. . . .

But she didn't rule out that it might be something more.

"Who's this?" Chloe asked, suddenly coming across a much more modern picture. In it a girl was grinning, standing with her arm around another girl, at the top of what was probably the Empire State Building. Old-fashioned quarter-operated binoculars, the kind that looked like giant silver robot heads, were blurry in the background, and there was something distinctly urban and gritty about the landscape beyond.

Kim leaned over, saw the picture, and cleared her throat.

"That's the girl who would have been your sister. If we are correct about your parentage."

"My *sister*?" Chloe held the picture closer. The girl was darker than Chloe and older; the date on the back indicated that it had been taken a few years ago, and she already looked like she was sixteen or seventeen. Her hair was the same as Chloe's, and there was a shape to her eyes that was similar; her nose was smaller, too. She had two fingers up in a V behind her friend's head.

Kim's exact words suddenly sank into her mind.

"What do you mean, 'would have been'?"

"She was the one I told you about who was killed by

the Tenth Blade. The pride leader's daughter. That would make you her sister," Kim said patiently, making Chloe feel like more of an idiot. "It happened several months ago. We think it was the Rogue."

"My *sister*," Chloe said again, feeling it on her tongue. Again she felt nothing in particular when she looked at the photo, but the word brought a swirl of emotions.

"Why . . . ?" she began. Tears sprang up in her eyes. It wasn't *fair*. She'd wanted a brother or sister *all her life* and it turned out that she'd had one *all along* and she'd been taken from Chloe, scant months before they would have found each other. It was so wretchedly, horrifically unfair.

"I understand she was a lot like you, actually. Or you if you had been raised Mai," Kim added thoughtfully. "I heard that she went out a lot by herself, doing a lot of things strictly among humans, and after her mother was killed, she was sent to live with her relatives, who were members of the New England Pride."

"There's a pride in New England?" Chloe asked. She remembered Kim mentioning the Pride of New Orleans, but colonial houses, white Christmases, and freaky cat people roaming quaint cobblestoned streets struck Chloe as strange. *I guess that's all relative these days, though,* she thought.

Kim just nodded, without explaining further. "I didn't know her very well. She was killed by herself, far away from her home, at night."

"Picked off because she was by herself," Chloe said

grimly. But something seemed familiar about what Kim had said—almost déjà vu. A dream she'd had, maybe: something about a girl running, panicked, in dark city streets. Being caught and having her throat slit.

"Yes . . . although the fact that it might have been the Rogue lends an interesting spin to the whole thing," Kim said, looking at the picture again. "To send someone like that out after her means they were pretty serious about *getting* her, which means they somehow knew she was the daughter of a previous pride leader."

"Do you think they know about me?" Chloe asked in a small voice.

"We still have no actual proof you are who we think you are," Kim said carefully. "So I would assume they have even less of an idea."

She imagined the man who'd attacked her running after this other girl, in probably the same fashion, running her down—without an Alyec or Brian to help save her. Maybe without so much of a fighting instinct. Killed by whirring throwing stars and tiny silver daggers.

"Why are they called the Tenth Blade, anyway?" Chloe asked.

"Because a pride leader has nine lives," Kim answered. "It takes nine blades to kill the One. The *tenth* is for the Tenth Blader if he fails."

Twenty-two

After she and Kim had made some preliminary plans for searching her house the next night, Chloe finally crawled off to bed, a thousand different thoughts and ideas crowding themselves into her brain. She had just drifted off, the pictures of her possible mother and sister laid out on the quilt in front of her, when Alyec showed up.

"Pssst! Chloe?" He knocked lightly on the door as he opened it.

Chloe blinked awake, then immediately sat up. *"Where were you?"*

"What?" Alyec asked, the eagerness on his face changing to dismay.

"I've been trying to call you. I tried calling you at home—"

"I was at a party," he mumbled, a little shamefaced about having fun while she was stuck here.

"Why don't you have a cell phone?" Chloe snapped.

"I do. Have one. *Had* one. Too many people started

207

calling, so I don't use it much anymore," Alyec said defensively.

"My mom—she's been taken. Kidnapped. Killed, I don't know." She sank back on her bed, trying to hold back the quiver in her voice.

He came over and sat on the bed next to Chloe and put his arm around her. "I'm sure that's not true."

"It is," Chloe answered dully. "I went to meet Amy and Paul—" She knew she should have said *and Brian* but couldn't deal with it right then. "And they told me no one had been home in a while. I went, and there's no sign she's been there for at least a week. She must have disappeared right after I came here."

Alyec hugged her to him, waiting a careful moment before asking the potentially inflammatory: "You went back home? After the last time you were attacked?"

"What would you have done if it was *your* mom?"

"I would go to Sergei and we would instantly round up a posse and—"

"Sergei won't do anything. Because she's *human*."

"Oh." Alyec seemed surprised by this. "What a dick-head."

Maybe this racial hatred thing is generational, Chloe thought. She hoped it was so.

"Why didn't you take me along?" he asked quietly. "I would have gone with you. You know how much I love breaking rules."

"It was something I had to do myself." *And it would*

have been pretty uncool for you to tag along while I was see-ing my other boyfriend. "Alyec," she said, sighing, "you get to go to school every day and do normal things with normal people in the outside world. I'm stuck here *all* day. *Every* day. Away from my mom and my friends and everything. I'm being . . . *cloistered* here." She gave her-self points for the SAT word.

"Kim seems to be okay about it," Alyec said, a smile on his lips.

"I love her dearly, but she really is a bit of a freak, you know?" Chloe ran her hand through Alyec's thick blond hair. "She said she would go back to the house with me and look for evidence or something."

"I will go with you, too," he said, kissing her on the side of her head, above her ear. "Screw Sergei. She's your mom. Hey," he said brightly, suddenly sitting back and looking at her, "this is the most naked I've ever seen you!"

Chloe caught herself looking down, forgetting what she had on. It was *completely* unsexy: a pair of blue-striped boxers Olga swore were new and an oversized, comfy, Old Navy men's T-shirt. The neck was so big it hung off one of her shoulders. Except for that little bit of *Flashdance*, Chloe didn't think she looked very naked at all.

"You have *got* to be kidding me," she said, holding her hand against his head to stop him as he reached for her. "I look like a frump."

"A *sexy* frump. A college girl, taking a break from her studies," Alyec said, evading her hand and kissing Chloe on her belly. "A *librarian* at home. You don't have any glasses, do you?"

"Alyec, shut *up*. Stop it!" She tried not to giggle. Her mom was gone, she had two boyfriends, she couldn't trust anyone. . . . "We're being *serious*."

"As a good librarian should be. Chloe, tonight the area will be crawling with Tenth Bladers because you were probably seen. No—definitely seen. You, me, and the freak will go tomorrow night and figure out what happened. Okay?"

"Okay," she agreed grudgingly.

He lifted the shirt up over her belly and pulled her boxers just the slightest bit down. Chloe was zinging all over as he brought his lips to her skin, both fearing and expectantly awaiting of his next move.

Which was to suddenly suck down over her belly button like a fish and blow air out the sides, making a ridiculous *thirbrrrrty* sound.

"Alyec!" She cracked up, hitting him over the head with a pillow.

"Chloe," he said, more seriously, kissing her. "everything's going to be all right. I *promise*."

Then he *really* kissed her. It was even better than their little time-out in the janitor's closet. He pulled her closer to him, sliding his hand up under her shirt. She felt the tips of his claws come out and pressed back into him.

"Al-yec!" came a booming male voice, pronouncing the name as Russianly as possible. Sergei stood in the doorway, hands on his hips, a growl on his face. He looked extremely leonine. "Do I have to establish a curfew in my own home?"

"Hey, she's part of this, too," Alyec said mock whiningly, sliding up and away from her in one quick movement.

Chloe wasn't sure whether to scream, cry, or giggle. This was such a classic situation—one that she had never been in before. Besides being scary and embarrassing, it felt sort of warm and nostalgic.

"Get *out*, Alyec Ilychovich," Sergei said, raising an eyebrow. There was a little bit of tired amusement in his voice as well. Chloe got the feeling that this was somehow not as bad as the whole sneaking-out thing. It was *bad*, but not unexpected, and not out of the realm of the legal.

Alyec slunk out after giving a brave salute to Sergei and blowing a kiss to Chloe. When he was gone, Sergei let out a sigh, a breath he must have held the entire time.

"That boy is a menace," he said wearily.

Chloe covered her mouth, pretending to scratch her nose, desperately trying not to giggle.

"I just came by to apologize," the older man said more gently, coming in and sitting on the edge of her bed. "I truly *am* sorry we cannot help your mother more. We should do everything we can for the woman who adopted you and brought you up and helped make you the wonderful girl you are." He put his square, stubby hand somewhat clumsily on her own. "But these are tough times . . . and the Tenth Blade is in strange agitation over you. I do not wish to risk lives—there are so few of us. Do you understand?"

When he looked at her with those large, white-blue eyes and that childish, hopeful expression, Chloe just wanted to hug him and tell him everything was all right. She *wanted* everything to be all right. She *wanted* him to have her best interests at heart.

But . . . Kim doesn't like him. What are her reasons? Chloe once again wondered. Actually, Alyec didn't really like him either. Olga was carefully neutral on the subject. The only person Chloe knew who admired him completely was Igor, Sergei's sort-of protégé.

He's not my real father, Chloe reminded herself. *Where the hell was Sergei when I needed to learn how to ride my bike or couldn't figure out how to multiply fractions or when Scott Shannon turned me down for the dance and asked Liz Braswell right in front of me?*

"I understand," she said, and it was sort of true. "I'm just sad. And I feel helpless."

"I know." He kissed Chloe on her forehead. "But remember, the Tenth Blade doesn't usually hurt humans. If they've taken her, she's probably fine, just a little shaken up. They're trying to lure you out, not hurt her."

She nodded, for some reason suddenly almost overcome with the urge to cry.

"Good." He patted her on the knee and stood up. "Are we on for a game of chess tomorrow? Lunch, maybe?"

"How about Scrabble?" Chloe suggested instead.

Sergei groaned. "Oh, good. A game designed for knowledge of English words. You just want to *win* for once, Chloe King. Okay, Scrabble it is." He grinned and left, his surprisingly thick and stubby legs rocking him out of the room. From the back he almost looked like some sort of alien from *Star Trek*.

As Chloe settled back down into her covers, she suddenly noticed the photos that she had left out on her bed. Had Sergei seen them? Would he care? Should she be worried?

Questions kept her awake for a long time before she finally fell asleep.

Twenty-three

As a kid, Brian had known there were secret rooms in the Order of the Tenth Blade's chapter house. As he grew older and advanced in the Order, some were revealed to him.

But he knew there had to be more.

And if the Tenth Blade was in fact holding Chloe's mom, they would probably keep her in some area Brian didn't know about.

As a kid, he had made incredible drawings and plans of where he thought the other rooms might be. While many of these floor plans were lost or had been destroyed by his father, a few had survived, stuffed into boxes of memorabilia and report cards. As soon as he got home from Chloe's house, he dug them out and pored over them, trying to remember what he could, picturing the old Victorian with eyes closed, estimating area and distance. When he had done as much as possible, he paid a visit to the house.

Mrs. Chung let him in, smiling and kind and looking exactly the way she always had from the first day he had been there. She was tiny but perfectly erect, grandmotherly but formally dressed, like the maitre d' at a fancy Chinese restaurant, her hair always up in elaborate pins. Whit Rezza might own a security company that constantly invented and sold the latest computerized systems, but in the end, few things could beat the watchful eyes of a *human* doorkeeper, one who was polite but firm with strangers, friendly with guests, and much better equipped than a computer to pick up the emotions of those who came in.

"Is everything okay, Brian?" she asked, looking as though she still wanted to pinch his cheeks.

"I'm having a sort of crisis of faith, Mrs. Chung," he sighed, telling her part of the truth. It was easier—and made it less likely that she would detect what he was up to—than an outright lie.

"Oh, I don't know about all that, but I'm sure it will be fine." She always claimed not to know what went on in the house whenever anyone—even members—tried to talk to her about it. She stood by the line that it was a private club. Brian doubted that she was really quite so innocent.

"Thanks, Mrs. Chung," he said as she took off his coat and went to hang it up somewhere.

Brian was well aware that cameras and monitors might be anywhere—he even knew where a few were. So he made his movements random—first to the library, where he said his hellos to a few of the older members who were sitting around reading or napping. He flipped through the latest *Sports Illustrated*—besides the dedication to violence, it really was, after all, an ordinary private club—and eventually rose, asking if anyone wanted tea or coffee. No one did.

He went to the kitchen, counting his steps, and poured himself a full cup of coffee to give himself an excuse for walking *very slowly*. Then he proceeded down the hallway to the stairs, counting his steps and trying to determine the length of the staircase.

While Brian did all this, he tried not to think of Chloe, partly because he was afraid it would affect what he was doing. And partly because it was too complicated to think about.

Five, six, seven, eight . . . About eight and a half paces to the stairway.

He had first been assigned to track her over a year ago; because of her adoption records, they had suspected that she was a Mai. He had tracked others before her, ones who already knew their heritage, and while it was never up to him to kill them—or decide to kill them—they always seemed different enough, alien enough for him to think of them as not quite human. Even discounting their greater strength and agility, they *moved* strangely, for one thing. Sometimes they cocked their heads when smelling for something, which made them look entirely animal. Late at night Brian had once caught a flash of a female Mai's face as she raced through a pool of streetlight and saw the catlike slits in her yellow eyes.

Chloe was just a normal high-school girl. Well, not quite normal. She was on the edge of the social crowds but never resentful of them. She had an amazing attitude toward work—Brian had seldom seen someone her age so committed to a crappy job. At least half the time Chloe showed up early at Pateena's and often stayed late to help the manager close up, without complaining or demanding overtime.

The Tenth Blade ordered him to get closer, to get a better reading on her and how close she was to discovering her background. He did as he was told.

He'd arranged their first "accidental" meeting at Pateena, the place where she worked. Liking her instantly was unavoidable: Chloe was funny, passionate, gorgeous, and had a spark of something else Brian couldn't put his finger on. Energy, verve, *something* that made him want to go everywhere with her, do whatever she was doing, not be left out in case he missed something great.

But he'd never counted on her liking him back.

Or having to decide how much to tell her. Or having to choose between betraying her or his father and the way he had been brought up, all the people he had known since he was a kid, the way of life he had always lived. In the end, he'd made a half-assed decision to come to her rescue at the bridge when she was fighting the Rogue without telling her anything beforehand. Not that she'd really needed his help.

And he'd screwed it all up again anyway. While there *were* Tenth Bladers waiting in the Marin Headlands for her to go running by, he hadn't *really* had to throw the shuriken so hard into Alyec's leg to stop them from going that way.

He *knew* that Alyec really wasn't the cause of the trouble—that one way or another Chloe would have realized she was different and, even worse, if she'd done it alone, the Order of the Tenth Blade would have simply killed her.

But the other boy could kiss her.

While Brian was forced to walk a strange tightrope with Chloe between friendship and something more, Alyec had no such difficulties. He was free to pursue any level of relationship with her, without having to worry about dying from it.

Brian was on the third floor, in a small complex of secret rooms where the *real* library was and where he was pretty certain there were *more* secret rooms, ones he didn't know about. He did a few quick calculations in his head and noticed how the decorative architecture was confusing, with excessive paneling and wainscoting, bookshelves set up in mazelike arrangements, lots of extra crown molding, cornices, and other random decorations.

A flash of something on the floor caught his eye. Brian bent over and picked up what could have been a gum wrapper. It was actually a silver earring. It looked expensive, patterned, and faux ethnic—and far too modern for anything Edna Hilshire would wear.

Brian quickly thought about all the other female members of the San Francisco chapter. Only two of them had access to this room besides Edna. Sarah-Ann never wore jewelry, except for a *Sodalitas Gladii Decimi* pendant, and Tyler always had a pair of simple diamond or pearl studs.

"What are you doing here?"

Of course. Of course Dickless would see me come in and follow me here. He was probably monitoring the security cameras.

Brian didn't turn around immediately, pretending to continue looking for a book.

The excuse he'd originally been going to use was that he had lost a knitting needle somewhere—his hobby amused some chapter members and annoyed some others, who thought it was unbecoming and housewifeish for a member of the Order of the Tenth Blade. Like flash camouflage, his answer would probably amuse or annoy an interloper, completely disarming any suspicion.

But Richard had a real grudge against him and still thought that the two were competing for Whit's affection and eventual leadership of the Order.

"Richard," Brian said formally, only turning around after he pretended to be done with whatever he was doing. "How are things going for you?"

"What are you doing here?" Richard repeated. His

eyes were black and intense, and his hair was black and intense, too. He sneered so much, it looked like he was constantly trying to stop a runny nose.

He was also smaller than Brian, which suited Brian just fine. Brian walked up to him as close as possible without making it an actual insult, looming over him.

"Not that it's any of your business, but I am experiencing a crisis of faith," Brian said, with just a touch of excitement in his voice to make it seem more real. "I wanted to read through the Sidereal Codex again and think about the vows."

"Don't you think it's a little late for that?" Richard demanded, retaining his sneer but obviously accepting the excuse.

"Remind me to tell the others that you're the go-to guy for spiritual support," Brian said, rolling his eyes and walking away.

"You can't just *leave* the Order," the other boy spat after him in a final attempt at ruffling his feathers. "*Nobody* just 'leaves the Order.' It's for *life*."

"Whatever," Brian called back.

"Even your father knows that, Brian. He understands the rules and lives by them. He'll do what's right. For all of us," he added.

Brian kept walking, but the smile he could hear in Richard's voice left him feeling cold.

Twenty-four

"Get anything yet?" Alyec needled.

"It would be a lot easier to 'get' a scent if you weren't wearing so much cheap cologne," Kim growled.

"It's not cheap! It's Eternity, by Calvin Klein!"

Chloe winced, fingering one of her mom's rings that lay next to the sink. The whole thing would have been funny if her mom's life wasn't at stake. Alyec seemed to rub *all* of Chloe's female friends the wrong way, not just Amy.

The three had escaped the mansion with little attempt at covering up their trail; with Kim's superior hearing and smell, they'd managed to eventually evade the two kizekh who had followed them. Alyec had crowed in triumph, but Chloe wasn't so sure it really had been just that easy; perhaps Sergei thought it was safe enough for her with Alyec and Kim.

Closer to Chloe's house Kim had detected two seemingly random people who, on closer inspection, were making fairly regular circuits of the area around the house. The three Mai simply waited until there was a break and dashed in.

"This is where you live?" Kim asked. Normally the girl was immediately down to business, but she seemed genuinely interested in Chloe's life before the Mai. She moved her head back and forth, taking in *everything* in the living room and kitchen, eyes wide at the coffeemaker, the little TV on the counter, the garbage cans, the books on the coffee table. . . .

"Yeah. Pretty sweet, huh?" Alyec threw himself down on the couch, making it clear that *he* had been there first and was much more familiar with the territory.

"This is where I found the . . . uh, 'clue.'" Chloe opened the fridge and showed her the hummus. Kim came forward to smell it, then buried her nose in her hand.

That had been fifteen minutes ago.

While Alyec made the occasional derisive comment and Chloe looked around for other, obvious out-of-place things that only she would be able to notice, Kim moved around the rooms, sometimes upright, sometimes on all fours, trying to catch a scent. She spent an inordinate amount of time with her nose close to, but not touching, objects, sniffing them—and Chloe couldn't quite watch. It was too inhuman.

"Here," Chloe said, slipping in between Kim and Alyec, who were glaring at each other. *I'm glad I have such great, supportive, helpful friends,* Chloe made herself think. *But maybe I should have brought only one of them.* She reached into a cabinet over the sink and pulled out a full bag of gourmet coffee beans—another sign her mother hadn't been there in a while. Normally she would have been through a "tasting"-size bag like that in about a week. She broke open the seal and held it under Kim's nose.

"What's this for?" Kim said doubtfully.

"They have little dishes of coffee beans out in fancy perfume stores and things like that," Chloe said, shrugging. "To clear your head of all the previous scents. I thought maybe you could use it for the same thing."

Kim looked at her without blinking but took a deep whiff. Then she wrinkled her nose and did the cutest little wheezy sneeze Chloe had ever seen a human—*Um, almost human*—do. She put her nose to the air again.

"Huh, it works," Kim said in wonder, and got back to work, taking the bag with her and glaring at Alyec.

"Hey," Chloe said, remembering something. "How come the night you were teaching me how to do all those things you reeked of gasoline, not CK?"

"Sometimes the Tenth Bladers use dogs," he said, making little ears on the sides of his head with his hands. "Gas covers the scent. Also to keep you from recognizing me. No one knew if you were going to freak out over everything. Like if you would suddenly start talking about all of this to your mom or the press or whatever—my name wouldn't be part of it."

"Well, I guess you guys lucked out about me, huh?" Chloe said dryly.

She watched Kim continue to sniff around the apartment. She wished she could do the same sort of thing—she had tried, but the overwhelming familiarity of the house doused all other scents. Kim would occasionally point to an area or a section of a door or something, but all Chloe got was a strange unfamiliar smell, mammalian, but she couldn't identify or distinguish it.

She wished she could do *something. Any*thing.

From the fight at the bridge to here, back home, a few things had changed. This time it wasn't Chloe who was in danger, but someone close to her. Last time she had been kicking a *trained assassin's* ass, feeling every blow bring her closer to victory. This time she was just standing here, uselessly watching someone else do the only thing she could think of.

Finally Kim stood up and shrugged. "There were two human males here and a woman who wasn't your mother. There are traces of fear and a chemical smell that I don't really recognize. . . ."

"O-kay," Chloe said. "But what does this mean?"

"It means that your mom was probably kidnapped, but the kidnappers didn't kill her. The chemical smell—it means they used something to make her pass out," Alyec said, leaping up and coming over to the two girls with a big grin. "It means that everyone's probably right about the Tenth Blade taking her to lure you out."

Kim nodded slow, grudging agreement.

"Well . . . now what?"

"Now we should go outside and see what else we can learn," Kim said, looking worriedly out at the street.

"You shouldn't worry about the two Gerbers out there," Alyec said, grinning. "I'll lure them away and get back here ASAP."

"Don't," Chloe said as he went to the door, even though she knew it was the best thing he could do.

"You think this is the *first* time I've done this?" He blew her a kiss and went out the back door, closing it silently as he went.

"We'll wait ten minutes and go," Kim suggested.

They were both quiet, watching the microwave clock.

"I'm gonna run upstairs and get some of my own, you know, undies," Chloe said after a moment.

"Can I come?" Kim asked shyly. "I'd like to see your room."

"Sure." Chloe shrugged. "C'mon."

She went upstairs, pushing her hands against the wall—something her mom hated—while Kim followed delicately behind. *If this was an actual friend-coming-over scenario, there'd be snacks on the table or popcorn in the microwave,* she thought dizzily. Here she was in her own house, late at night, her mom having "disappeared," toting a cat-eared girl who seemed as anxious as a freshman to see how the cool kids lived.

Chloe went to her dresser and began to look through its drawers, trying to disturb things as little as possible.

Out of the corner of her eye she saw Kim looking around, eyes wide, paws spread as if she would like very much to *touch* something. Chloe wondered what the other girl's room looked like: probably bare and ascetic, like its owner. Not covered in posters of Ani DiFranco and Kurt Cobain and Coldplay, not filled with IKEA furniture, not strewn about with Mardi Gras beads and scarves and other useless sparkly crap.

Chloe had found Monday, Tuesday, Wednesday, Friday, and Sunday of her Paul Frank panty-a-day collection when she heard a slight hiss from her friend.

She turned just in time to see Kim dive with a speed and movement completely unrecognizable as human.

When the girl stood up again, she had a mouse between her thumb and forefinger.

"It looks like the vermin have already taken over in your absence," she noted, holding the mouse above her head and eyeing it critically.

"That's Mus-mus," Chloe said, putting out her hand, claws extended, and gently but firmly taking the terrified mouse from her. "He used to be my pet."

Kim let it go, fascinated.

Chloe cupped her hand around the mouse with her claws so he couldn't get out. He was obviously terrified. Any hope that his fear of her was temporary disappeared. When she'd developed claws and her other Mai attributes, he'd become as scared of her as he would be of any cat.

"A cat with a mouse as a pet," Kim said, almost sounding delighted. "Weird, but kind of ironic."

"I thought we were lions," Chloe said, crouching and letting him go again under her bed. She fished in his old drawer for some more Cheerios to leave out for him. At least he had decided to stick around. She should be grateful for that much.

"Well, then there's that fable about the mouse who begged the lion who caught him to let him go."

Chloe vaguely remembered the story but not the details. She tried to concentrate on it so she wouldn't cry again over Mus-mus.

"The lion let him go, and later, when he had a thorn in his paw, the mouse pulled it out. They became friends after that."

"What's the moral?"

"Do kindness to even the least significant creatures—it may wind up helping you far more than you imagine sometime down the line."

"Sounds a little self-serving," Chloe said, finally turning around and jamming the undies into her pockets.

"Perhaps." Kim cocked her head at her. "Who knows what thorn of yours Mus-mus may pull out?"

"I think we can probably go now," Chloe said, suddenly uncomfortable. Kim nodded and waited politely for Chloe to exit first, following her silently downstairs, through the house, and out the back door.

Once outside, Kim crouched down in what would

have looked like an impossible position to balance in if Chloe hadn't known herself what it was like to be a Mai. The other girl tracked the sky and then the ground like a werewolf out of a very, *very* bad movie. Black against the dim light of the street she was skinny and beautiful, and for a moment Chloe felt a pang of envy.

The Kings' and their neighbors' tiny patches of "yard" were separated by a fence and dwarf privet trees that grew out of brown, unhealthy-looking dirt.

Chloe's mom did not exactly have a green thumb with outdoor plants. Whenever she came across a pretty landscape in a magazine that might work with their minimal space, she would hold it out to Chloe, who would look at it and grunt. Sometimes there would be a trip to Home Depot or a nursery, things brought back, and diggings begun, but then Anna would take on an especially heavy caseload and would recede from the project, muttering something about hiring someone to do it.

Chloe suddenly grew depressed when she saw a bottle cap and some gum wrappers stuck to the ground under the trees. Her house was empty; without its two occupants—its soul—it was nothing more than a monument to crappy urban living. She had to resist the urge to bolt.

Kim had come crawling back to her, looking irritated and confused.

"Well, it was definitely cased before they came in—I got a perfect scent trail of the two male humans."

"And?"

Kim carefully cleaned off her claws, polishing them with the edge of her jeans. As prim and feline as it looked, it was as obvious as if a human were doing it that she was trying to delay an answer.

"And?"

"There were Mai. Two of them. Slightly younger trail. *After* the humans, but not by much."

"Oh." Chloe thought about this. "I guess Sergei sent them to guard my mom, without telling me, to keep me from getting upset."

"If Sergei had sent two Mai to guard your mom and three humans showed up, your mother would still be okay, safe in her house, even now. The humans would be dead or incapacitated," Kim said. It was obvious she had already come to her own conclusion, and its implications darkened her brow.

"What are you *saying*?" Chloe grabbed the girl's shoulders, wanting to shake her out of her neat little world of logic and puzzles. "That they were sent to *kill* her?"

"It wouldn't be the first time. . . ." Kim trailed off.

Chloe fell back on her heels. "No!"

"There is no real evidence, but—"

"Why haven't you told me this before?" Chloe demanded.

"Because everything is *watched* at the house and *every*one listens!" Kim hissed. "I have tried to tell you that a *thousand* times!"

"Does everyone hate humans that much?" Chloe asked dully as her universe shifted.

"It is not about hating humans—it's about control and keeping the Pride together. The Path of Bastet involves doing it with connection, love, nurturing, and purity. The Path of Sekhmet means doing it through war and violence, by any means possible."

"And the current leader is a follower of Sekhmet," Chloe realized, thinking about what Sergei had told her.

"Once your mother is gone, you have no more connections to the outside world."

Chloe smiled weakly. "That's what Brian said."

"Who's Brian?"

"He's my—" Chloe stopped, unsure of how much to reveal. "He's a friend of mine in the Tenth Blade who saved me, sort of, when I was fighting the Rogue and then when Alyec and I ran away. . . ."

It was Kim's turn to stare in incredulousness.

"Your life," she observed finally, "is very complicated. And extraordinarily dangerous."

"Tell me about it." Chloe looked at the blank eyes of the house, its dead windows. "So—you think my mom is dead?"

Kim shook her head. "If she was killed by the Mai, there would be signs. We aren't perfectly neat killers. Ironically, it may be a good thing that the Order of the Tenth Blade—or whoever—got to her first."

"Hey, guys, stop with the chatting!" Alyec poked his

head into the bushes where they sat. "We have about five minutes before they figure out I led them on a wild-goose chase."

He put out his hands and helped the two girls up. Chloe was surprised that Kim didn't object, but the girl still seemed a little stunned by the evidence and their discussion. As they walked back, just three normal-seeming teenagers, Kim filled Alyec in on what she had found.

"So we think she's been kidnapped by the bastards?" Alyec asked excitedly.

"She's probably still being held somewhere by them, yes. Assuming it is the Tenth Blade and not someone else, for some different reason," Kim said. "If it *is* them, your little diversion with their guards tonight may have bought us some time—it proves to them that Chloe is interested, or *someone* is interested, in coming back to this house. Which means they have a reason to keep her mom alive."

"Excellent," Alyec said, rubbing his hands together. "We can have a real raid! I'll bet Sergei knows where their HQ is. . . . This is going to be great! There hasn't been any real action in years!"

"I hardly think the leader is going to sacrifice a troupe of us and the kizekh to attack the home base of the Order of the Tenth Blade to save a woman it looks like he was meaning to have killed."

"Maybe we can embarrass him into it," Alyec posited.

"Pride leaders don't embarrass that easily, Alyec,"

Kim objected, with the faintest gleam in her eye. "I think we should look to volunteers. There are enough who think we've been too intimidated by the Order for years and are just itching for some payback."

"I wonder how many we can get."

"I wonder how we can avoid too much death and injury."

As her two friends animatedly discussed and formed plans, Chloe remained silent. In the streetlights, their three shadows climbed the empty street before them, doubled, and then receded into the light of the next to be reborn slowly again behind them. They could have been Amy, Paul, and Chloe for all the detail their gross shades gave them. Just turned away from a party or something, planning great revenge, or discussing their dreams, filled with the sort of energy only walking on the streets at night can give you.

Instead of making war counsel.

"Hey, are you all right?" Alyec asked when they got back. Chloe still hadn't said a word.

"Yeah. I'm just a little . . . tired." She couldn't even smile weakly at him. "It's a lot to think about, you know? I thought Sergei was like—"

"Your dad?" Kim prompted quietly.

"And now it looks like he was just going to kill—"

"All the fun, if he catches the three of us skulking around," Kim interrupted what Chloe was about to say, looking obviously around with her eyes. Chloe understood immediately. No more talking. *Not here.*

"I should get home, anyway." Alyec kissed her sweetly on the lips. "I'll come back tomorrow after school and we'll talk about this more, okay? What to do about your mom, I mean," he added pointedly. While Alyec had seemed a little aghast at what Kim had accused Sergei of, he, too, didn't seem particularly surprised. Between the family enmity and his desire to maybe take over someday, the boy was all gung ho about disobeying the leader—and possibly punishing the older man somehow.

Chloe waved good night to him and Kim and went upstairs.

Hours later she was still awake. The photos were once again spread over her quilt as she sat huddled against the headboard, knees drawn up to her chin. Sometimes Chloe would pick up a picture, like the one of her sister, and hold it in front of her face for a long time, staring at it like she was trying to see the 3-D image in one of those trick posters. She tried to *feel* the other girl through her face, tried to pick up some sort of impression or thought across the void. Then she would put the picture carefully back down in the exact same place it had been.

Her photo quilt was missing quite a few panes: there should have been pictures of her mom, Amy and Paul,

Marisol from the shop. All the people she hadn't really been related to but who felt like family had been slowly replaced with people whom she was probably related to but knew little about. Kim and Olga. Igor and Valerie. Even Sergei. And what about Brian and Alyec? If things continued the way they seemed to be going, Brian and Alyec might be literally facing off in a few days.

She thought about her mom, who hadn't known what she was getting into when she'd decided to raise Chloe on her own.

Amy's walkie-talkie buzzed.

"Hello?" she asked distractedly, still staring at the pictures.

"It's Brian. Look . . . I can't talk much now." He was panting as though he were running, and Chloe could hear street sounds in the background. "Listen, I was just over at the . . . Order's place and found an earring. Does your mom wear big blocky silver things with patterns and black in the etchings. . . ?"

"John Hardy," Chloe said calmly, both shocked and unsurprised. "Does it kind of look like animal plating? Like of a snake? Or like spheres that have been squished flat, almost into polygons?"

"Bingo. I don't think anyone in the Order wears anything like them."

"Can you . . . can you get her out?"

"I don't even know exactly where she *is*, Chloe. And people are becoming suspicious of me over there.

If we tell the police, it will amount to nothing—my dad's *very* experienced in avoiding that kind of trouble." There was a long pause. "Chloe, if you are planning some kind of raid, you should know—it's going to be a bloodbath."

Chloe didn't say anything.

"Some people have been waiting years for this kind of direct confrontation. And while the Mai may not carry weapons, we do."

Chloe felt trapped and uncertain. "Have you told Amy and Paul?"

"Not yet. I'm meeting them in a few minutes to give them back their walkie-talkie—they're very possessive about it. Maybe the three of us together actually *can* think of some way of extricating your mom secretly. Anyway, three heads are better than one. And your friend Amy seems pretty experienced at the whole hacking and breaking-and-entering thing."

She smiled at that. "All right. Thanks. Keep me posted."

"Will do!"

Chloe hung up and put the picture of the Mai woman back on the bed with the others. Then she flipped open the phone again, dialed Brian's home number, and waited.

"Hi, this is Brian Rezza—if you're looking for Whit Rezza, you can reach him on his cell at 415-555-1412. Leave a message. Thanks!"

She hung up. Then she dialed again, carefully remembering the number.

"Hello?" A rich, masculine voice answered the phone.

"Hello, Mr. Rezza. It's Chloe King." She paused for a long moment, working up the courage to speak her next sentence. "I want to talk to you about a trade. Me for my mom."

Twenty-five

Chloe waited on a rock in the middle of the Presidio, obviously by herself and open to attack.

This was one of the most central, hidden areas in the mazelike complex of abandoned army buildings, a long-empty row of houses that were small and neat and as kept up as a suburban dream—but completely empty. The grass was trimmed on the little shared green the houses all looked out on, and the rock on which Chloe sat had obviously been moved there from somewhere else. Lucasfilm was moving its headquarters or something there at some point; for now, the area at dusk was as weird and perfect and lonesome as a Tim Burton set.

Chloe sang a little song to keep up her spirits, but all she could think of was "New York, New York." It still had a lot of 9/11 connotations to it, patriotic and stirring—fitting for her current mood in the empty military base. But her voice was reedy and got lost in the wind;

she kicked her heels like a little girl and waited for something to happen.

As the breeze changed direction, she caught a scent. *Human.* A few of them. And something familiar—a warm scent, a comforting skin smell.

"You can come out here," Chloe called carelessly. "I'm all alone." She tried not to get too excited, but they really *had* brought her mother with them. The exchange would happen. And no one would get hurt. Except for maybe herself.

Whit Rezza stepped out of the shadows. He wore a long, flowing raincoat that made it look like he was about to get on a plane for Europe, not negotiate for the release of a captive. Following him was a younger man in khakis and a black leather jacket, propelling her mom forward with a gun to her head.

"Chloe!" her mother said, trying to cut the sob of relief into a direct order. "Get out of here. These people are insane."

"No can do," Chloe said cheerfully. "It's my fault that all of this stuff is happening, and I'm going to fix it."

"Chloe, leave this *instant*," her mother said again, standing up straight and looking over her glasses at her.

"None of this would have happened if you hadn't adopted me," Chloe said.

Her mom rolled her eyes and almost stamped her foot. "Chloe, would you *shut up*? I *love you* and I'm *your mother* and I'm *telling you* to run away while you still can!"

"How much did he tell you?" Chloe demanded. "What did he tell you about me?"

"I told her the truth," Whit said. "Well, up to what she could handle."

"He told me that there's some sort of Russian Mafia connected with your biological family and they're involved in . . . I don't know, bad crimes or something, and that they had lured you in. And that they needed to protect me from them—that they would come after me. And that you had been involved in a murder. Whatever the story, this gentleman has a *gun* to my head, so I'm guessing that the truth is a bit skewed."

"You never believed anything we were telling you?" Whit asked, a little surprised.

"Piss off," Chloe's mother spat.

Her daughter couldn't help grinning. "Don't worry, Mom, it's for the best."

"You would do well to listen to your daughter," Whit suggested mildly. "For a member of the Mai, she is surprisingly logical."

"Yet you're *still* going to kill me," Chloe said, rolling her eyes.

"You killed a member of our Order."

"I did *not*. I tried to *save* him," Chloe said, leaping down from the rock, frustrated.

"Yes, that's what my son keeps saying."

"That's because it's the *truth*!" Brian stepped out from around a building, throwing stars ready in his hands.

"Brian?" Chloe said, surprised.

"Brian?" his father said, confused.

"Brian," Richard spat. "I should have known you were going to try to save the cat bitch."

"Don't talk to my son that way," Mr. Rezza snapped, surprising everyone.

"Since when does the Order start carrying guns, you coward?" Brian demanded, coming closer, eyes locked on the other young man's.

"How did you know I was here?" Chloe asked, relief washing over her. She still had every intention of saving her mom and keeping the bloodshed to a minimum, offering herself up as a sacrifice—but she was also extremely grateful that there suddenly might be options other than her possibly being killed.

"I didn't. Once I was pretty sure that they had your mother, I kept an eye on my dad and followed him and Dickless here."

Brian didn't look like the brooding, complicated man she knew; he strode forward confidently, never taking his eyes off the gun, every inch the hero she wanted him to be. The wind blew his thick dark hair back, and his face was livid with anger.

"I *saw* her reach her hand down to try to save Alexander when he slipped—with my own two eyes!"

"But *why* would she do that?" his father asked, sounding genuinely confused and a little exasperated.

"Because she's a *good person*, Dad."

"You saw that when you were at the bridge *helping* her," Richard said, jerking his chin in Chloe's direction. "I'll bet."

"Yeah. That's right," Brian spat. "Sue me for trying to help an innocent girl you sent a *psycho killer* after."

"So the betrayal is complete," Mr. Rezza said wonderingly. "Of the Order, your forefathers, your own father, your mother—"

"Don't you *dare* bring Mom into this," Brian yelled, aiming one of the shuriken at his dad.

"I cannot—will not protect you from whatever action the Order takes against you," his father said levelly, not looking at the weapon targeted on him. "Or random acts of revenge." He said this to Brian, but his eyes flicked toward Richard.

"Will you *listen* to yourselves?" Chloe said, suddenly weary. She had watched the whole fight between father and son in silence and finally couldn't take it anymore. "Kidnapping innocent people . . . hired assassins . . . revenge and protection and betrayal and weird secret societies that go from generation to generation. It's insane! Both you *and* the Mai. This is America in the third millennium. *AD.* Leave all that other shit back in Europe and the Dark Ages where it belongs. You think of yourselves as self-appointed protectors of the human race, but you're nothing but a group of barely restrained vigilantes waging a war on people who never did anything to you!"

"The Mai killed my wife," Whit began, with great emotion.

"No, they didn't. Brian told me. She was killed on a raid that *you* sent her out on."

Chloe's mom turned to look at Whit. "You lied even about that? That's *sick!*"

"She wouldn't have *been* killed if a human hadn't been attacked and killed by the Mai, forcing us to call the raid—"

"Okay, just stop," Chloe said, throwing up her hand. "Each side can claim a million random violences done back and forth on them—"

"Since the Slaughter five thousand years ago, when you wiped out an entire country of humans," Whit interrupted. "And I will *not* be talked to by a teenage girl, Mai *or* human, like that. As for 'random violences,' Miss King . . ." He stepped forward as he spoke, glaring at her. "While luring you out of hiding was important, we've done this to *protect your mother*—who was as good as dead the moment you took up with Sergei."

Chloe's eyes widened.

"Oh yes," Whit chuckled, "I know Sergei. And his habits . . . Did you know that male lions, when they take over a pride, often kill all the cubs fathered by other cats?"

That gave Chloe pause.

"We kidnapped your mother for her *own* sake. To keep her safe."

"It's amazing the lies you continue to tell." Sergei

came tapping up the previously empty road, his expensive shoes echoing against the pavement. Behind him were seven deadly looking Mai, all trained kizekh. Unlike a troop of humans, they didn't march in unison: they prowled and sniffed the wind and kept their unblinking slit eyes on the enemy.

"There are four more hidden behind the house and two over there," one of them hissed to Sergei. "They reek of machine oil. . . . They must all have weapons, guns, except for the two behind that bush."

"I suppose this was inevitable, wasn't it, Sergei?" Whit said easily, turning from Chloe as if she were dismissed. Richard tightened his grip on Mrs. King.

"Nothing is inevitable," Sergei replied crisply. He cocked his head, and two of the Mai disappeared into the shadows to take care of whoever they found there. "Since when has the Order stooped to kidnapping innocent women?"

"As soon as you sent out assassins to kill her, you murdering animal!" Brian's dad began to lose his cool; black anger shone in his eyes.

A gunshot went off, muffled, somewhere among the houses. No one jumped except for Chloe. There was a thump and a growl somewhere else—like they were in the middle of a horror movie, with horrible things happening all around them in the dark.

"Um, was this little secret meeting of mine secret to *any*one?" Chloe asked, partly of the world, partly of

Brian. Mostly it was a failing attempt to lighten the situation. She had tried to fix everything herself and avoid a fight—and what she'd done was bring the opposing parties together, armed, at an out-of-the-way place where no one would have any idea what was going on.

Young, feminine screaming—and a not-so-feminine male shriek—came from the bushes.

"Wait! We're not sworders—uh, Bladers—don't hurt us!"

"Amy?" Chloe said, recognizing the confused voice. Two of the kizekh slunk into the open, one with an iron grip around Amy and Paul.

"They're with me," Kim said, stepping out of the darkness. Alyec was next to her, cursing in Russian and wiping blood off his arm.

"How did you . . . ?" Chloe looked at them in wonderment. *Everyone* really was here.

"I am the best tracker in the Pride," Kim said, drawing herself up straight.

"And the walkie-talkie I gave you?" Amy said, stepping carefully away from the scary-looking soldier with his mouth open and canines bared. "It's got GPS."

"We knew where you were every minute. We tracked you on it." Paul was camo-chic, in army pants and a tight-fitting camouflage windbreaker.

Chloe had a thousand questions: How had they all gotten to know each other? How had they gotten together? How had Amy and Paul reacted to Kim? How were Kim and Alyec getting along?

But most of all, she felt like sobbing in relief. All of her closest friends had come to help her out. To save her.

"Paul, Amy, go *home!*" Mrs. King ordered. "You too, Chloe. I don't know what the hell is going on, but you need to get out of here."

"The deal was Chloe for you," Whit said, pulling his attention away from the four new teenagers and back to Sergei. "We are prepared to let that deal continue, no questions asked, no blood, everyone goes home safely."

"You're trading a woman's life for that of her own *daughter?*" Brian said bitterly. "I guess I should have seen that coming. After Mom . . . I should have known."

"You shut up, Brian. I've had just about enough of your lip about your mother for this lifetime," his dad growled. "You're unworthy to even speak her name."

"Ah, father and son." Sergei sighed. "I do so love the warmth in human families."

"What would you know about that?" Richard demanded, jamming his gun into the side of Anna's face for emphasis. "Don't cats screw anything that moves and then move on?"

"You'd better muzzle the child, Whitney. Don't let him start what you can't finish," Sergei said, waving his hand in the air. It was clawed. Chloe wasn't sure if Brian's dad understood what that meant: that he was just about ready to attack.

"*Finish?* Like when you *finished off* entire villages—"

"That was five thousand years ago," Kim pointed

247

out as calmly as possible. She and Alyec had slowly put themselves in between Amy and Paul and the rest of the people there. Amy bobbed her head around so she could watch what was going on; Paul just looked confused.

"Um, yeah." Chloe cleared her throat and spoke up. Just to let people know that she was still there. Wasn't *she* the reason everyone was here tonight? *No, I'm just an excuse,* she realized, looking at the fanatical faces around her. Both sides were itching for a fight, a real one, after years of uneasy sort-of truce in this country. Led by two middle-aged leaders who felt they had something to prove.

"Maybe we can talk about this," Chloe's mother suggested, also as calmly as she could. "There seems to be a long-standing dispute between your two groups here."

Chloe was horrified to see tears running down her mother's cheeks—of fear or pain as the gun was jabbed into her temple, she wasn't sure. *My mother.* Something inside Chloe finally snapped.

"Sir! Ramirez is down!" A young man wearing an outfit similar to Richard's came running forward with a gun, four neat lines of blood across his face. "We were attacked from behind—he's bleeding badly, sir. But we got one of them *good.*"

"A preemptive strike, Sergei?" Whit demanded, pulling a short, curved sword out of his coat.

With a snarl, the female kizekh who had been arguing with Kim leapt at the soldier.

Ellen, her name is Ellen. Chloe had watched *Star Wars* with her just a few evenings before. She was completely Mai now, eyes slit and fangs bared and tearing into the young man like he was paper.

From then on everything happened in slow motion.

Silently, Richard took the gun from the side of Chloe's mom's head and pointed it at the lion woman. Almost in aftereffect, muffled blasts afflicted Chloe's ears, three bangs, one after the other.

Brian immediately made for Richard, a look of raw hatred on his face.

Amy and Paul looked at each other, confused, then Amy screamed ever so slowly; Chloe couldn't make out the words, but she and Paul began to run.

More Tenth Bladers came out of the night. Chloe was stunned by their numbers—at least a dozen; far more than the kizekh had thought. They must have been hiding downwind. Why had Brian's dad brought them all? It was just supposed to be her and him. Even the dickhead holding the gun to her mom's head was a surprise. . . .

As in a bizarre instructional film about reproduction, each Tenth Blader found a Mai, each Mai found a Tenth Blader, and they all began throwing weapons or struggling in the dust. Even Kim and Alyec. The look on Kim's face—white-eyed horror turning to rage as someone attacked her, as if she couldn't quite believe it. Alyec tried to shove her out of the way. . . .

Chloe didn't know what to do.

She had come here to save her mother. And now what? What *could* she do?

No one was attacking her; the struggle was going on inches from her feet, the very one she'd been trying to prevent.

Sergei neatly avoided Whit's attack with the knife, moving far more agilely than a man of his age should have been able to. Before Brian could reach Richard, Sergei brought his square hand full of claws down like it was a giant paw and cuffed him squarely on the side of the face; Richard fell down instantly, and Sergei neatly retrieved the gun as he did.

"Nobody move!" Sergei demanded, spinning around and leveling the gun at Mrs. King. "Call off your men, Whit, or I'll shoot your captive."

Chloe couldn't quite believe what was happening. It made sense—the Tenth Bladers would do anything to protect a human, but still . . . was he serious?

Paul and Amy froze; Mrs. King did, too.

Suddenly Chloe had a path, a thing to do.

She ran, sprinting for her mom. That was why she was there.

"No!" Brian screamed, and made for Sergei. "Leave her alone!"

And Sergei fired.

It could have been meant for Brian, or it could have been meant for her mom. Chloe would never know. All she was sure of was that this was her fault, her doing. She dug a claw into the ground and pushed herself forward.

There was very little pain when the bullet first entered her flesh.

But when it hit her heart, it was like her entire body caught on fire.

"Chloe! No!"

She had no idea who was screaming: It could have been male, female, or a number of people.

She crumpled to the ground.

Her heart was very loud in her ears, and the ground was very cold under her head. The rest of her was on fire, as though she were being burned alive.

She listened interestedly to the muted sounds around her and the slow thumping of her heart.

After a few more beats, it stopped entirely.

Twenty-six

Blackness. Echoes.

The sounds of something distant that might have been water dropping, but thicker. Wind howled somewhere, but no breeze touched her face.

Chloe recognized where she was even before she opened her eyes.

She was farther back from the edge of the cliff than the first time, when she had come to this place after falling off Coit Tower. Far below was what looked like a pool of mercury that bubbled and rippled uncertainly.

She noticed things she hadn't before: directly overhead there were millions and millions of stars and galaxies and strange planets she couldn't have named, far more terrifying than the emptiness she had thought was there. It was like she was at the end of the universe, the end of everything.

Something screamed, low and insistent. When she squinted, Chloe could just make out shadowy forms flickering in and out of sight, just beyond her vision, impossible to hold for more than a second. Like they weren't there—or like they were an optical illusion.

Chloe backed away to the edge of the cliff, putting as much distance between them and her as she could.

"Chloe. *Saht.*"

It was a whisper, a purr, and a growl all combined.

One shadow hovered closer than the rest, lingering.

"Daughter."

"M-mom?" Chloe asked, quavering. The shade had no recognizable form, slipping back and forth from something vaguely bestial to something upright.

"Now you know your destiny. Go back."

"But wait—what is this?" Chloe asked desperately, trying to grasp at things she knew in her heart were fleeting and impermanent. "Where am I? What happened to you?"

The shadow wavered and shifted, like there was extremely hot air between them.

"Return to your living mother. She is reality now—as I am, in your past."

Chloe didn't understand. She opened her mouth to ask something more, but a rush of hot air hit her on the chest like a fist. Chloe flew backward off the cliff, into the darkness below.

Life, when she returned to it, was pain. She reached into her chest with her claw and with an agonized groan pulled out the bullet that was lodged there. Blood poured down her front and slowed to a trickle as she watched. Soon it stopped entirely, and she felt an itching where the skin and sinew began to knit.

Sounds began to make sense around her, not that she cared. Murmurs of, "She is the One!" and, "Why isn't she dead?" and just, "Chloe!" from the people who simply loved her. The fighting seemed to have stopped; several of the Mai were on their knees before her.

Her mother was beside her, making sure she was okay.

No, wait—her mother had carefully angled herself *between* Chloe and the Tenth Bladers, shielding her daughter with her body. Whit's men shifted hesitantly on their feet, starting to raise their guns and then dropping them, unsure what to do.

Shakily Chloe got to one knee and then rose from there. It hurt every part of her, but she stood.

"*Any*one," she said, loudly and evenly so everyone could hear her, "human *or* Mai ever touches my mother again, I'll *kill* you. I will hunt you down and kill you. And I have seven lives left to do it in."

Chloe put her hand to her side, which still burned. She leaned over a little to ease the pain, facing Whit and his remaining Tenth Bladers. "Listen to me: I did *not* kill the Rogue. He fell off the bridge when I was *trying to help him back up*. I have never hurt *any*one. Neither has Alyec or Kim, or Paul or Amy. *Or my mom.* You can all leave us out of your little war."

Amy and Alyec ran forward when she began to sway,

255

each throwing one of her arms over their shoulders. Paul and Kim followed.

"As for the Mai . . ." She looked directly at Sergei. There was no proof that he'd actually sent assassins after her mother, but he was the second person that evening to train a gun on her. "Home isn't Mai or human. Home is home. And I'm going home *now*."

She put out her hand and her mom took it.

Clasped, unnoticed in her other hand, was her mother's silver earring, the one Brian had found. She looked back at those they left, the wounded, the dead, the respectful Mai, and the confused humans.

Brian was not among them.

Chloe, her four friends, and her mother walked quietly out into the night.

Twenty-seven

Two Mai and two human teenagers sat in a booth at the Washington Diner, silently drinking coffee or hot chocolate, picking at a large order of cold, greasy fries topped with thick bright ketchup that reminded everyone there too much of blood. The fluorescent lights made everything harsh and lifeless. The late-night waitstaff was grumpy and standoffish, which was fine for the four gathered, who had no urge to socialize with strangers.

Alyec, Kim, Paul, and Amy sat uncomfortably, like distant cousins long separated at a family reunion told to go make friends with other kids their age. Kim had borrowed a scarf from Amy and wrapped her head with it like a babushka, hiding her ears. The waitress had just rolled her eyes—she was used to the late-night freaks who came in.

"So . . . ," Paul said, playing with a fry. "What does this whole . . . being-the-One thing mean?"

Kim had her paws wrapped around a mug of hot

chocolate and was staring into the depths, looking spacey even for her.

"It means she is the natural leader of this pride. That her mother was probably the previous leader and that she, like her mother, fulfills all of the traditional requirements: loyalty, bravery, compassion, fair-mindedness, and a willingness to come up with solutions to seemingly impossible situations." Kim pulled herself together a bit, falling into her usual didactic role. "It means that her ka is true and noble and that she would do anything to defend her friends and family. It means she has nine lives—or seven now, as she said. And other . . . less definable traits."

Paul and Amy nodded mutely, and even Alyec seemed interested in the subject, like it was news to him.

"It means Alyec is no longer next in line to be leader," Kim said carefully.

"That's okay; too much responsibility," Alyec said, trying to be humorous—but it came off sounding bleak. Even he wasn't untouched by the events of the night.

"From what you've said, it sounds like that Sergei guy should no longer be the leader," Paul said slowly. "That it really should be Chloe."

Kim nodded mutely and looked back down at her hot chocolate.

"Did you see those two old freaks?" Amy spoke up, voice wavering. "It was like Mr. Rezza and Sergei were off in their own little world. . . . Did you see how he

258

treated Brian? Like either *one* of them is likely to give up power. *Ever.*"

"I have never seen violence like that before," Kim said into her mug, then looked up, wide-eyed and shocked, like a child. "I've seen fights and duels, but . . ."

Alyec nodded, leaning on his hand. "I know. I thought it would be *fun* or something."

Paul and Amy looked at each other. Paul reached out his hand and squeezed hers.

"We didn't end up doing *any*thing to help her," Amy finally said, frustrated. "We were supposed to be doing all this detective legwork crap, and none of it mattered. . . ."

"If it wasn't for your idea with the walkie-talkie, we never would have found her," Alyec pointed out.

"We were there." Kim looked up at all of them. "Supporting her. I think that sometimes, that's enough."

"One thing's for certain," Alyec added, stirring his coffee with a claw. "Her life is going to get even more complicated and a lot more dangerous from now on. . . ."

Twenty-eight

Chloe and her mom sat on the couch, mostly silent. It had taken over an hour just for Chloe to tell her mother the story and another hour for Mrs. King to ask the inevitable questions.

Mrs. King got out some expensive scotch and downed a shot. She offered Chloe some, but Chloe declined, wanting cocoa instead. Mrs. King made it for her, going through the movements robotically.

"Oh, here's your earring," Chloe remembered, taking it out of her pocket. It gleamed dully in the light. She turned it over in her fingers, staring at it. "It's so random. . . . Such a tiny chance that it fell, and that Brian found it."

"Give your mother a *little* credit," the older woman said with a wry smile, indicating how *both* of her ears were bare. "Every time they moved me, I dropped another piece of jewelry or whatever, hoping it might provide *someone* a clue as to where I was. I think I'm out

261

about three thousand dollars' worth of the stuff." She handed Chloe her cocoa and shook her head.

Chloe smiled—it was still too soon to grin. *I really do have the coolest mother.* She couldn't imagine Mrs. Chun or Amy's mom thinking to do something like that. But her face darkened again as she thought about moms and the other thing she had to tell hers.

"I saw my biological mother," she said after they had been silent for a while. "When I was, uh, dead."

Mrs. King looked up at her through slightly glazed eyes—dim from the evening, not the drink. There were bruises and scrapes on the side of her head where the gun had been jammed against it. Her usually pixie-perfect hair was tousled, and her glasses were bent. Chloe wished she didn't have to see her mother this way—she might have thought her mom was a perfectionist bitch sometimes, but seeing her like this was almost unbearable.

"What did she say?" her mother asked after a moment.

"She said that she was proud of me and that I should go back and rescue you—that you were my real mother, too."

It was a difficult thing to say, but Chloe was glad she had.

Even when her mom began to cry and hug her.

They finally said good night, somehow both knowing it was safe for now. Chloe had meant every word she had said about killing whoever tried to attack her home again, and the Mai seemed to respect her now. And the Tenth Blade had something to think about.

She wearily climbed the stairs to her room, wanting desperately the hot, cleansing water of a bath but too exhausted to seriously consider the effort of running the water or waiting for it to fill.

Chloe sat on her bed, empty of all thought, trying to kick off her sneakers without bending over to untie them.

She was startled by a tap at the window.

Brian was there, his frame obscuring a surprisingly clear night full of stars. Chloe felt her stomach lurch for a moment when she saw him. There was blood on his face and hands; where he tapped, an ugly dark blotch remained.

Chloe leapt up and pushed open the window.

"Brian!" she cried. He was holding his shoulder, like there was a wound there.

A bullet wound, she realized, catching a faint odor of metal and powder. It smelled like poison to her, like death.

"Hey." He smiled weakly. "I'm all right. Nothing too serious."

"Come in—I can get some bandages. . . ." He was balanced on the outside of the sill as neatly as if he were Mai, and she was afraid he would fall if he lost too much blood.

He shook his head. "I can't. I just came to say goodbye."

She didn't understand; it was all over. The good guys had won—and he was a good guy.

"Why? What's the—?"

"I'm a dead man," he said wearily. "Richard is basically calling a fatwa on me—as a traitor to the Order. And my father refuses to protect me. You never quit the Order while you're alive."

"But you had no choice! You told me! Your father made you."

He shrugged. "It doesn't matter. I said my vows when I was fourteen—and now I'm a wanted man. I have to disappear."

Finally Chloe began to cry, streams of silent tears coursing their way down her cheeks.

"Brian, it's not *fair*. You were just trying to *help* me. It's all my fault. . . ."

"*Nothing* is your fault, Chloe." He reached in and grabbed her hand, squeezing it. "Nothing is your fault. You're good, kind, and smart. . . . I have no doubt that you'll make a great leader to your people." He looked her seriously in the eye. "But you know that you're a top to-kill on the Order's list, right?"

"I know," she said sadly.

"My hanging out here would only put you in more danger, Chloe." He took his hands off hers and began to stand. "I love you," he said, and kissed the glass near her face.

She leaned forward and kissed him back, the cold glass between them keeping him safe from her.

Then he fell into the night, disappearing into the city.

Chloe covered her face with her hands and wept.

Epilogue

Sergei sat at his desk, hands clasped under his chin as though he were praying. He had run a claw through his hair, fixing it, but there was blood on his cuffs from when he had taken down one of the younger members of the Order, pulling at the tendons in the boy's neck while closing his fingers.

It had been a long time since Sergei had personally gotten involved in a fight. He had missed it—there was something incredibly stirring and visceral about protecting your people with your own body. That was one of the signs of a real leader.

A real leader knew what to do during peacetime as well, knew how to manage a modern bureaucracy to gather his people safely, to work the system and reunite families and keep them all employed and safe and hidden. He had done exactly that for the past fifteen years or so. *I am a leader,* he told himself, *and no one is going to take that away. Certainly not some little girl from San Francisco.*

He opened a drawer, using his claw to undo the lock, and took out a small, nondescript gray cell phone. He dialed a number with his thumb, claws receding.

"Hello, Alexander? First, let me offer my condolences," he said with a chuckle, "since everyone seems to believe that you are dead.

"In other business, I thought we could help each other out again. Remember the pride leader's daughter? The one you, ah, *took care of* with my . . . *assistance*? It turns out she has a sister, Chloe King. Yes, you've met—Yes, she's the One. . . .

"And I can help you find her. So you can take care of *her* as well."

Chloe King has

~~9 Lives~~

~~8~~

7

6

5

4

3

2

1

New from Simon Pulse

Check out this exciting excerpt
from the second book in the

quartet by Jeff Mariotte.

FALL

Kerry had just shut the journal and replaced the leather thong that held it closed when Sonya and Dougie entered, arm in arm, laughing at some joke Kerry wasn't privy to. "Hey, Kerry," Dougie said by way of greeting. "That doesn't look like any textbook I've ever seen. What is it?"

"It's an old journal," Kerry replied, not wanting to reveal any more than that. Dougie annoyed her—she considered him a typical frat boy but without the frat, all about using his college years to drink and party and have a good time, knowing that at the end of it his degree and his father's connections would guarantee him a good job even if he never set foot in a classroom. She didn't quite know what Sonya saw in him, but then she didn't know Sonya well enough to speculate.

He disentangled himself from Sonya and reached for it. "Lemme see."

Kerry jerked it away from his grasping hands. "It's very old," she insisted, "and fragile."

Dougie screwed his blunt, good-old-boy features into a mask of hurt. "Jeez, I wasn't gonna damage it," he declared. "I just wanted to look at it."

"Kerry's pretty protective of her stuff," Sonya told him. Kerry noted her tone, as if she were talking about someone who wasn't in the room.

"Just the stuff that needs protecting," she countered. "This journal is almost a hundred years old, and the paper is brittle. I can't let anything happen to it."

"It's okay, Kerry—chill," Sonya chided. "No one's going to mess with it. Dougie's just having fun."

"More than you are, it looks like," Dougie added. "Looks like you need a boyfriend, Kerry. You shouldn't be sitting around here on a Saturday night with some moldy old book."

"You don't have to worry about me," Kerry answered, wishing he'd just go away.

She sat on her bed and picked up BoBo, her old childhood rag-doll clown. "I'm fine."

"Tell you the truth, Kerry," Sonya said, dropping her voice to a conspiratorial level, "we were kind of hoping you had gone out for a while, if you know what I mean."

Sonya's meaning couldn't have been more clear. *But do I want to do her that favor?* Kerry asked herself. *Do I want to clear out of my own room so she and her horndog boyfriend can have their fun . . . and maybe paw through my stuff— even Daniel's journals—when they're done?*

Resigned, she gathered up the things she'd need to spend an hour in the common area. For about the millionth time since the semester had started, she wished she had a private room.

By the time she had settled on one of the couches in the third floor lounge, Kerry was fuming. Two girls she knew vaguely shared another couch and spoke in hushed tones about a project they were working on together, but blessedly the TV was off and the faint smell of microwave popcorn that hung in the air when she entered dissipated quickly. She made it clear that she was there to study, not socialize, and she buried herself in the American history text that she should have been reading instead of Daniel's journal. The words seemed dry and lifeless to her, though, especially compared to the journals, or even more, to Daniel's voice, telling her things about her nation's past that had never made it into the history books.

Kerry was trying, really and truly, to immerse herself in school, to put Daniel and Season and the rest of it behind her. And Kerry was someone who did what she put her mind to—they hadn't called her Bulldog over the summer for nothing. So why couldn't she just focus on the work? Why did images of Daniel pop up, unbidden, every time her mind wandered? Why did she keep seeing Season in every blond woman on campus?

The whole situation was just incredibly frustrating. She turned back to the history text and tried to read about the landing at Plymouth Rock, but the words just turned to fuzz before her eyes.

Daniel was there, in her dream, looking just as he had in life. His long-sleeved white shirt was clean and crisp, tucked into faded jeans, the sleeves rolled back a couple of times over muscular forearms. His hair was long and windblown, and he was laughing, head thrown back, mouth open, teeth even and white, gray eyes crinkled at the corners and dimples etched into his cheeks. He stood on a hill, at a slight distance from Kerry; she couldn't reach him or even hear his laughter, which should have been booming.

She moved closer to him, or tried to. But for every step forward she took, the hilltop on which he stood seemed to move back. She tried calling out to him, shouting his name, but even her own voice vanished before it reached her ears.

Then a fog rolled in, as if from offshore—thick and wet, blotting out the view, blocking Daniel, then the entire hillside. Within seconds Kerry was alone, an island in a sea of white mist. Then even she was gone, the mist breaking her body into ever smaller chunks until it had disappeared completely.

Kerry Profitt's diary, October 21.

And again with the nightmares, now. All I need, right? Having gotten rid of them once—thanks, I am now convinced, to the appearance of Daniel in my life—they are back, and, it seems, with a vengeance. This one wasn't even all that scary in itself—I mean, the imagery wasn't—but the overall feel of it creeped me out big time. Especially the way that Daniel was there, and then he wasn't, and . . .

Oh, never mind. It's different from the dreams

I used to have, which I forgot as soon as they ended. And a year from now I won't remember what the dream was, and this entry will make no sense.

Which distinguishes it from the rest of my life how, exactly?

Now Sonya is sleeping hard and I am wide awake, pretty much giving up on the idea of sleeping tonight. Fortunately the laptop screen gives off enough light so I can type without turning on a light and waking her highness. And since it's fresh in my mind, I can't stop thinking about the dream.

Its meaning? Obvious, I think. I miss Daniel. He was taken from me. Duh. Bonehead psych, no brainer.

The part where I disappear? A little tougher, that. Losing my identity? Maybe.

And maybe I should e-mail Brandy for a more comprehensive analysis. She's the Doc, after all. I have her addy—we all have each other's, and have sent a few around since splitting up back in SD after the summer. But not as much as I thought we might, almost as if everyone wants to forget what happened, wants to leave Season and Daniel and the summer of our discontent well behind.

And really, who can blame 'em for that? It pretty much sucked. Find a great guy, and he dies. Find out witchcraft is real and scarier than you ever imagined, and the baddest witch around has it in for your new BF. Find out he's been chasing her for almost 300 years, so you help him catch her, only to watch her kill him.

Yeah, summer means fun.

Okay, here's the thing. School is just not happening for me. Sonya . . . ditto. Aunt Betty and Uncle Marsh check in from time to time, but I could be gone from here for a month before they knew it. So really, what's keeping me here? Lack of someplace better to go?

Only, see, I have an idea about that too.

I've been reading Daniel's journals. That's just about the only thing that's held my interest, in fact. And Daniel is lost to me.

But that doesn't mean that part of my life has to be lost. Mother Blessing is out there, in the Great

Dismal Swamp. Season Howe is out there too, still at large, and now owing for yet another crime.

One that I take just a little bit personally.

So here's my theory. I find Mother Blessing, convince her to teach me witchcraft, and then I hunt down Season Howe and give her what she deserves.

Nothing to it, right?

But did I mention people call me Bulldog?

More later.

K.

As many as 1 in 3 Americans
who have HIV... don't know it.

TAKE CONTROL.
KNOW YOUR STATUS.
GET TESTED.

To learn more about HIV testing,
or get a free guide to HIV and
other sexually transmitted diseases:

www.knowhivaids.org
1-866-344-KNOW

1-800-WHERE-R-YOU

A series by Meg Cabot, writing as Jenny Carroll

She can run, but she can't hide.

Just because her best friend wants to exercise, Jessica Mastriani agrees to walk the two miles home from their high school. Straight into a huge Indiana thunderstorm.

And straight into trouble. Serious trouble.

Because somehow on that long walk home, Jessica acquired a newfound talent. An amazing power that can be used for good... or for evil.

Run, Jessica. Run.

From Simon Pulse
Published by Simon & Schuster

3085-01

FEARLESS™

THE END OF AN ERA IS NEAR. . . .
BE AFRAID.

YOU'VE WATCHED GAIA BREAK LEGS.

YOU'VE WATCHED HER GET HER HEART BROKEN.

BUT YOU'VE NEVER SEEN HER
BREAK FREE QUITE LIKE THIS.

GAIA'S HIGH SCHOOL DAYS ARE NUMBERED.
AND ONCE THEY'VE RUN OUT, GAIA WILL
MAKE HER MOST DANGEROUS CHOICE YET.

DON'T MISS THE FINAL ADVENTURE
IN THE BEST-SELLING SERIES:

AVAILABLE NOVEMBER 2004

AND COMING SOON:
FEARLESS FBI

PUBLISHED BY SIMON PULSE

Check Your **PULSE** Book Club

Sign up for the CHECK YOUR PULSE
free teen e-mail book club!

★ **FEATURING** ★

A new book discussion every month

Monthly book giveaways

Chapter excerpts

Book discussions with the authors

Literary horoscopes

Plus YOUR comments!

To sign up go to www.simonsays.com/simonpulse and
don't forget to CHECK YOUR PULSE!

BODY OF EVIDENCE
Thrillers starring Jenna Blake

"The first day at college, my professor dropped dead. The second day, I assisted at his autopsy. Let's hope I don't have to go through four years of this...."

When Jenna Blake starts her freshman year at Somerset University, it's an exciting time, filled with new faces and new challenges, not to mention parties and guys and... a job interview with the medical examiner that takes place in the middle of an autopsy! As Jenna starts her new job, she is drawn into a web of dangerous politics and deadly disease... a web that will bring her face-to-face with a pair of killers: one medical, and one all too human.

Body Bags
Thief of Hearts
Soul Survivor
Meets the Eye
Head Games
(with Rick Hautala)
Brain Trust
Last Breath

BY CHRISTOPHER GOLDEN
Bestselling coauthor of
Buffy the Vampire Slayer™: The Watcher's Guide

Published by Simon & Schuster

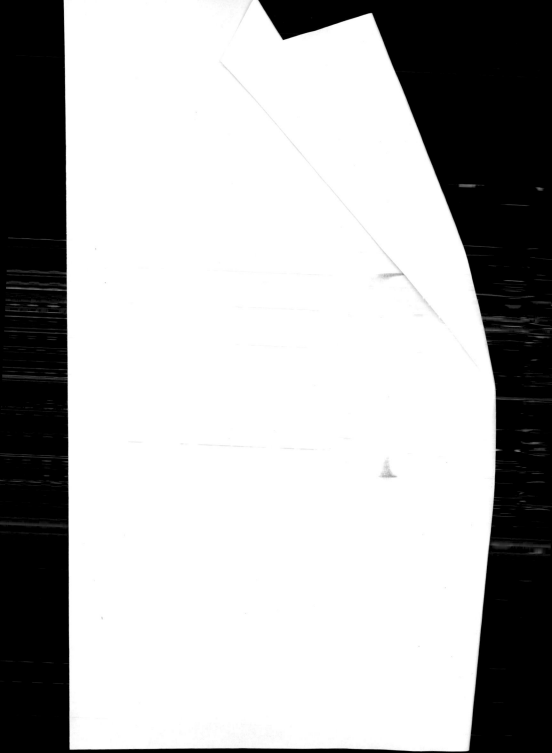